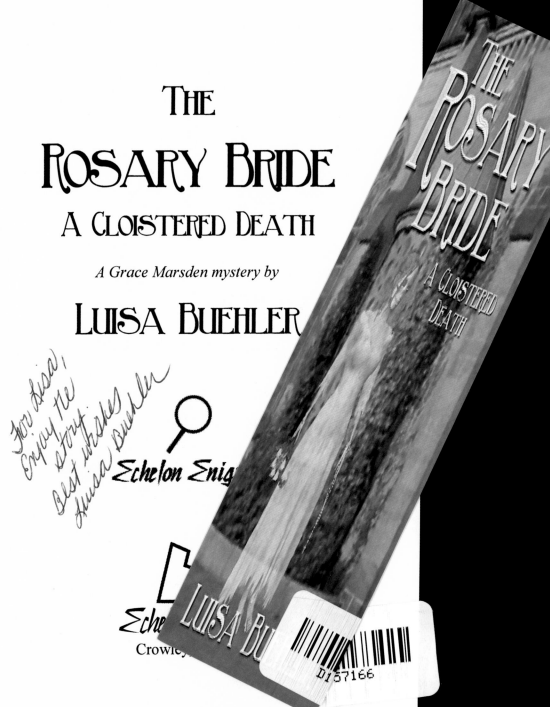

THE
ROSARY BRIDE
A CLOISTERED DEATH

A Grace Marsden mystery by

LUISA BUEHLER

For Lisa,
Enjoy the
story.
Best wishes
Luisa Buehler

Echelon Enig

Eche
Crowley

D157166

Echelon Press
P.O. Box 1084
Crowley, TX 76036

Echelon Enigma
First paperback printing: May 2003

Trade paperback ISBN 1-59080-227-6

Printed and bound in the United States of America.

www.echelonpress.com

Praise for Luisa Buehler
and
THE ROSARY BRIDE

"...a twisty, taut, compelling story of love gone wrong, a fascinating, haunting tale."

> --Carolyn Hart, author of *Engaged to Die*

"...a stylishly written novel evocative of Barbara Michaels...an engrossing tale of old wrongs, long-kept secrets, and murder."

> --Denise Swanson, author of the bestselling Scumble River Mysteries

"A taut and suspenseful whodunit laced with a healthy dose of the supernatural. A chilling debut."

> --Lee Driver, author of the Chase Dagger Series

"My favorite kind of book--old sins cast long shadows. When a long-dead woman is found behind the fireplace at Regina College, new crimes begin to happen. *The Rosary Bride* is suspenseful and poignant."

> --Barbara D'Amato, author of *White Male Infant*

"Everything you could want in a mystery. Murder, mayhem, and more. The Rosary Bride will have you begging for more in the series!"

> --Alexis Hart, author of *Dark Shines My Love*

DEDICATION

The Dominican nuns at Rosary College taught me to care, to dream, and to persevere. They encouraged academic excellence and spiritual balance. I dedicate *The Rosary Bride* to that community of women and to my husband Gerry and son Christopher who encouraged me with their patience and love as I wrote these many years..

CHAPTER ONE

Barely muted by the crash of shattered stone on wood flooring, a shouted expletive reverberated off the high ceiling of Regina College's stately library. Sudden silence gripped the room as a dozen heads swung simultaneously to stare wide-eyed at the two red-faced tradesmen planted toe-to-toe in front of the massive stone fireplace. The taller of the pair, a beefy fellow with hard eyes and a stubborn chin, stood bunched in a boxer's stance, his right arm cocked, his hand balled into a fist. The shorter man held his ground, but he seemed more shell-shocked than ready to fight. Shoulders drooping, he cradled a heavy hammer to his chest as he gazed slack-jawed at the rubble littering the floor around his boots. Unnoticed by either man, a fine film of masonry dust hung in the air between them and encircled their heads like misty halos, the final product of a now gaping wound in the back wall of the fireplace.

In that frozen moment in time, I heard a slight rustling sound followed by a *click, click, click.* As if on cue a small glass bead rolled out of the jagged hole and tumbled to the floor.

The spell was broken as quickly as it had been cast. Hurrying forward, I dimly heard the questioning voices of my friends as I pushed between the two men and bent to retrieve the tiny bead. Another bead trickled from the wounded masonry and joined its predecessor on the floor. One more hung on the edge of a gray shard like a tear poised to drop. I knelt down to pluck it from the rubble.

The assault on my senses began immediately. A puff of cold, dank air long imprisoned in the wall pushed against my face in search of freedom. My stomach tightened and the hair on the back of my neck scraped against my collar. I wanted to turn away; I was drawn closer. My jaw tightened and bits of my breakfast rocketed to my throat and stopped just short of gagging me. Head pounding, filled with noise and motion, I saw what they couldn't see; what I'd never forget. Suspended in the dark hole, as if in a desperate stretch to the light and perhaps the touch of another, dangled a bony hand.

I screamed and pulled back. The room seemed to tilt and shift my focus from the gaping hole up to the chandelier twenty feet above me and back again.

"Gracie, what's wrong? Grace, what is it?" Strong arms lifted me to my feet and pulled me back from the fireplace. Someone placed a chair behind my wobbly legs. I sat down quickly and clamped my knees together to keep them from shaking.

"Call Ric. Call Ric now."

"Ric. What are you thinking? What's..."

"Call him, now. There's someone in there."

My announcement of entombment caused a minor uproar. Gasps and shouts amid a building crescendo of questions filled the air around me. People began pushing and moving.

Don Rakin's soothing voice could be heard moving through the chaos, calming pockets of people as he moved among them. He was tall, six feet, six inches but his stooped frame hid his height, as the oversized sweater and baggy khakis hid his slender build. His pale blue eyes blinked more than usual even for him. He was the coordinator of the library move and in that capacity, he took charge. He asked us to move away from the crumpled structure.

The pounding in my head diminished. I looked around. Karen stared at me. I smiled weakly and saw relief on her face. Don pushed a glass into my hands. I sipped the icy water. The clean taste filled my mouth, easing the tightness in my throat and erasing the cotton dry taste of fear. The gaping hole drew everyone's attention. Several friends moved closer to me. Sitting on the chair, I had a lower sight line. I could see some white lacy material. My shoulders twitched and I looked away.

I stared into the water. My hands automatically sought the chain of yarn I always carried somewhere on my body. I pulled a bright red length from my pocket and began a memorized pattern of loops and twists. Immediately the familiar process soothed my jangled nerves. My adrenaline flow ebbed and my stomach seemed to retreat to an area closer to my waist. Curiosity overtook my initial fear and I looked back toward the hole. It wasn't a pleasant sight, but I had really come unglued. I usually handled shock better than this histrionic display. For some reason, this felt different. I was still shaking.

"Who's Ric?" A second shock seemed inevitable.

"What?" I turned to look at Doreen.

"Who's Ric? You told Karen to call Ric."

"I told her to call the police," I corrected her.

"You told her to call Ric. You didn't say anything about police."

My face flushed hot. My head pounded with renewed ferocity; I turned away from her and walked the length of the library toward the doors. Ten feet before the exit I made a sharp right turn, passed the abandoned circulation desk and stopped at the door to a windowless room housing thousands of periodicals and magazines shelved on metal racks.

I glimpsed my reflection in the window in the top half of the door to the room. My shoulder length, dark brown hair seemed more tousled than usual even for me. Lavender eyes with flecks of gold and an expression of fear, maybe panic, something not normal, stared back at me. I pushed the door and moved past my image. The area I was in was referred to as the stacks. I stopped to take a deep breath. My lungs filled with the delicious smell of old and new words blending and living on paper. The saying, 'so many books, so little time' caused a smile. I inhaled deeply again and continued to walk through the stacks for another twenty feet before I reached the exit. Now I was in an alcove at the back of the building. In the 1940's, there had been three small dormitory rooms and a hall with direct access to the Sisters' dining room and the college chapel. During a renovation of the area, the two rooms at the far end had been remodeled into a reading room for the nuns. A long narrow hallway led to the remaining old dorm room. The door and part of a wall to that room had been removed to make a study alcove for students in Power Hall. The long hall and partial room made half a *cul de sac*. Students used it as a shortcut from the dorm to the library or to the chapel. No one ever studied in there. The room had never been comfortable; it had always been the coldest spot in the building.

Felt fine to me. Right now this was what I needed, a haven from that terrible scene in the library. Not many people traveled all the way down this corridor anymore. They usually cut through closer to the Sisters' reading room.

College legend persisted that a lonely spirit haunted the alcove and nearby hall. As far back as the forties, students talked about seeing a beautiful girl in a flowing, white dress carrying a luminescent white rosary in her hands walking into the room at the end of the hall. That section of the building housed the oldest dorms. No one had been assigned to those rooms in years. Even after the renovation students still claimed that they saw the beautiful specter in fancy dress enter the alcove. She always carried the shimmering white rosary draped over her clasped hands, as though in prayer. Some said they called out to her and followed her but when they flipped on the light, no one was there. I had heard all the stories when I was a student here. By that time, girls had named the ghost the 'Rosary Bride.' No one I knew ever saw her; no one I knew ever came here alone.

My fingers found the rough texture of my yarn and began to work the ends round against themselves and back again over the middle while my mind tried to deal with what had happened in the library. For the umpteenth time, I mentally thanked my mother for providing me with a simple way to calm my nerves and focus my thoughts.

During my early childhood, my mother had recognized the constant braiding, plaiting, and twisting of anything I could grab as the behavior of an obsessive-compulsive personality. I braided an assortment of string, dandelion stems, rubber bands, twist ties, and ribbon. Mostly, I twisted my hair to the point where clumps of it would come out. My mother became frantic when I had no fewer than three bald patches about the size of nickels. At that point, she channeled my 'jitters' as we called them into finger braiding using yarn. I was never without a length of yarn. I jittered more when I was stressed or scared. In my job as an editor of children's books, I never encountered anything scarier than alien green globs or misguided witches.

Until now. So, why was I sitting alone being stressed? I was also an alumna of Regina College. It was the commitment to that part of my life that prompted me to volunteer to help move the existing pre World War II library into the newly constructed Rebecca Crown Resource Center. The grand old room could no longer accommodate the rising enrollment since the college gave up its women only status and opened its doors to men. For that reason I found myself in this predicament braiding as fast as my fingers could twist.

Traffic had been nonexistent this morning when I zipped eastbound on the Eisenhower Expressway. Even the 'Hillside Strangler,' the bottleneck at the merge had posed no threat to my schedule. The drive through River Forest on familiar side streets brought me here in no time. I parked near the Fine Arts Building and followed some other blue jeans clad 'thirty-something's' into Lewis Hall.

This morning the lobby outside the old library served as a staging area to tag, feed, and direct the alumni work force. We formed a ready group gathered by flyers, phone calls, and guilt tactics by class agents. The alumni office decided that a liturgy should precede the breakfast. Mass at Regina was always a warm, friendly experience.

The Chapel smelled of polishing wax and well oiled wood. Mixed with those smells was a touch of mustiness that lived in every old building with a past. Three-foot thick stone walls kept the Chapel cool and quiet. The cacophony of college life had seemed to stop at the heavy oak doors, as though the concept of sanctuary existed for all who entered. I never forgot the peacefulness I felt each time I stopped in for a chat with God.

My husband, Harry, and I often drove in from our home in Pine Marsh, a Western suburb near Naperville, to enjoy the camaraderie of Sunday Mass. Although he was raised in the Church of England, Harry appreciated spirituality in any setting.

The mass this morning had been even more special since I shared it with women I hadn't seen in ten years. The occasion had mushroomed into a working reunion of sorts. Some alum had decided to stay a few days and were sharing hotel rooms or bunking with old friends still living in the area. Friendly smiles and quick nods crisscrossed the intimate chapel. 'Pass the peace,' our term from college days, took longer as we moved among the pews and hugged seldom seen classmates. I saw Karen Kramer across the chapel and moved to join her after the final benediction. We had shared all of our English classes together and had discovered we were kindred spirits.

Karen who was blessed with a tall, slender, athletic build was my physical antithesis. She wore her curly, dark blonde hair very short. Dark brown eyes, framed by large tortoise shell glasses gave the appearance of wisdom, wit, and intelligence. I always teased her and told her without her glasses she'd be just a blonde. She really was the only one with whom I had stayed close - we were best friends.

The friendly atmosphere in the Chapel spilled out into the second floor of Lewis where we enjoyed coffee, chitchat, and croissants. The old library was to become a beautifully detailed study hall. The room had a twelve-foot ceiling all around the perimeter with a center ceiling that peaked to twenty feet. Ten chandeliers divided the long room and provided basic illumination.

Studying there had always been a romantic, brooding experience. It seemed all the English majors studied in the Library. Science majors labored in well-lighted areas. They probably realized the damaging effects to one's vision from squinting at badly illuminated pages. I thought it was necessary to read *Wuthering Heights* in the atmosphere of a dimly lighted, drafty Great Hall. I believe I understood the ambiance of the English novel because of this old library. The alcoves created by the lower bookshelves, had since been fitted with spot lighting, which wrecked the mood, but saved the vision.

My team, Karen Kramer, Doreen Ripler, and Marietta Doyle, was assigned bookcases #16-#20, next to the fireplace. I had always tried to sit near the fireplace and had often imagined what it would have been like to study by the light of a blazing fire, reading about Heathcliff and Cathy searching for each other on the cold unforgiving moor while I sat warm and safe until only the red hot embers in the heavy metal grate remained.

That fantasy had never happened since the fireplace sat empty and cold throughout the four years I attended Regina. It hadn't housed a log since the early 1960's when structural damage left it dangerous to use. Since the library was being repainted and furnished with comfy chairs and reading lamps, Mary Pat Lanigan, a trustee from the class of '52 decided it would be nice to have a working fireplace.

Some workmen were already chipping around the front of the mantle. The stone work with the original inscription was to be removed and affixed in the new library's foyer for the dedication in two weeks. The ceremony was planned for the same Sunday in December as when the current library had been dedicated all those years before. This fireplace would then be fitted with a gas starter, glass doors, and a blower motor to make it more fuel efficient and cost effective. Would Heathcliff mind?

We worked in friendly closeness exchanging small talk on kids, careers, and significant others. Our task was to remove the books from each shelf, wipe them off with a specially treated cloth designed to clean and hydrate the covers. The next step was to shelve them on rolling carts to be taken to the new library. After ninety minutes, we were ready for a break and Karen offered to go for coffee.

During that entire time we had been subjected to the constant bickering of the two men hired to relocate the mantle. They argued about the process they should use. They argued about the tools they would need. They cursed the bricklayer since apparently the original installer had taken no shortcuts. He had mortared and cemented every inch of the structure not just the contact points. The argument escalated into a shoving match as a small crack in the firebox widened into a gaping hole when one worker lost patience. Each blamed the other for the damage. The final culpability was laid at the feet of the original artisan for doing too good a job. He obviously had never intended this fireplace to be moved. Had he known its secret?

My heartbeat kicked into high gear as I remembered the 'secret' I had glimpsed in the crumbled masonry. The memory spun my thoughts to another anomaly, namely, the Rosary Bride. I shivered.

"Dammit, Grace, you came in here to think about seeing Ric again, not fifty year old ghosts." I lectured myself aloud. "Why did I tell Karen to call Ric?" I continued speaking to no one. "Maybe he won't be on duty. Maybe he'll assign someone else to investigate. Why did I ask for him? Can't start again. I don't want to be here."

I couldn't keep my thoughts sorted and suddenly I knew why. The room was freezing. I don't know how but in the last ten minutes it felt like the temperature in the alcove dropped at least twenty degrees. The deep cold seemed to make the room brighter as though the frigid surfaces reflected the light more intensely. There was something else too. No, someone else. I had the uncanny feeling that someone was in the alcove with me. That was impossible.

A slight sound, a rustle like lace against lace seemed close by. A freezing chill moved slowly down my spine to my lower back until I couldn't move my legs. Goose bumps erupting on my arms were the only movement my body could manage.

I heard a soft breathy sound like someone expelling breath to form the hard 'gr' of my name. I felt frozen to the chair. I didn't want to see her if I couldn't run. I sat perfectly still and waited. The sound came again. This time stronger, not a distant motor kicking on, not a door swishing shut down the hall. It was my name.

"Grace? Are you all right?"

Karen's voice and my scream sounded simultaneously.

"My God, Grace, what is it? You look like you've seen a ghost."

How could I tell Karen she wasn't far from the truth? "Nothing. You, ah, startled me. I was thinking."

"You're shivering. Let's go back to the library. It's freezing in here. I was worried about you," she said as she took both my hands. "Wow, your hands are like ice. Here, take my sweater." Karen insisted on bundling me up in her woolly Pendleton. The sweater was a classic, and a shade of ivory that happened only to very old and very expensive wool.

"What made you come here? I wouldn't have walked down this far if I hadn't seen the light blazing from the room. You know I never liked walking down this hall. Even now, it gives me the creeps. C'mon let's go."

What did guide my steps? Or who? Today had begun without a hint of the events that would shatter the calm of a beautiful fall day and challenge my resolve to keep my marriage intact.

CHAPTER TWO

We returned to the library to find people still gathered in small groups, their heads bent together, talking in whispers. Some watched a uniformed police officer cordon off the area blocking the entire fireplace. He was winding plastic yellow tape around the backs of chairs he had positioned to secure the crime scene. One of the chairs he used was the one I had sat on. My empty glass was on the floor near the hole.

"I'm surprised you asked for me." The quiet statement came from behind me. I turned to face his voice. I pulled the collar of the sweater closer to my face as though woven fabric could act as a barrier from the voice that had haunted my dreams and filled my thoughts for too many years. I looked up at the most handsome man I had ever met.

Ric Kramer, at six feet four inches tall, would be an imposing figure by anyone's tally. In addition to height, he possessed a physique *to die for,* as my niece would say. His appearance implied strength. His personality demanded respect. Ric's chiseled features were straight, clean, and incredibly sexy. Thick dark hair and coal black eyes made it damned near impossible not to stare. He was also a police inspector.

Deep parts of a person's subconscious never forget or turn off. They wait for a tiny flaw, stress fracture, glitch, or whatever, to appear in the wall they have so carefully and painfully built around their feelings. Then, in a moment of vulnerability, emotions burst through and that wall becomes so many pieces on the floor just like the fireplace that started all this. I had bullied Karen into calling the one person I should never have seen again. My hand tugged abruptly at the length of yarn in preparation for the next moments.

"Grace, are you all right?" His voice sounded concerned and heavy with feeling. "Karen said you demanded she call me?" Ric's question was tentative.

How could I explain the shattered wall in my subconscious? I could only stand and look into the blackest eyes I had ever seen and remember how deep into his soul I once had looked. The officer who had accompanied him saved me from answering.

"There's a skeleton in there all right, Inspector "

"I know that. That's why we're here, Sergeant."

"I just meant to confirm what was reported"

"Sergeant, if Mrs. Marsden reported a skeleton, then there's a skeleton." He made that last comment looking directly at me. Somehow, the 'Mrs. Marsden' was a shade too tight. Maybe some of the hurt was already flooding back. Maybe *his* wall was starting to crumble.

"Yes sir," replied the officer. Ric turned abruptly and issued a few brief words to the Sergeant. Now Inspector Kramer turned a charming and reassuring face to the anxious alumnus.

"Would everyone please pick up their belongings and move out of the area. We can't allow you to continue working in here for a while. Don't worry Sister Joan," Ric said, with a glance at her nametag. "We'll keep you informed. Now, please, if you could make sure everyone leaves the library. Thank you."

I moved to retrieve my bag from the table.

"Mrs. Marsden, I'll need you to stay, for a statement, if you don't mind." His voice was casual but the shaded tone bothered me.

"Ric, Grace really didn't see anything. Those idiot workers broke the..."

"Karen, I understand that you were out of the room when Grace, ah, Mrs. Marsden made the discovery. I won't need you to stay."

"I'm staying with Grace." Karen sat down and folded her arms across her chest.

"Fine. Stay quietly then, will you please? Thank you."

Ric's tone dismissed his sister to a corner of his mind. This was the attitude, the tough and sometimes hurtful disposition that made him so successful. He'd used it to become one of the youngest detectives to make the rank of inspector.

"Now, Mrs. Marsden?"

That damned 'Mrs. Marsden.' So clipped, so precise.

"A statement?"

"Ah yes," I stammered. "Of course, Inspector Kramer." My voice gained strength as I gained confidence. So be it. I could be just as precise and formal. Before I could say anything else, the same officer approached us. Ric bowed his head to insure the shorter man's confidentiality and listened for a few seconds. The news seemed to annoy him as he cut off the whispered conversation by abruptly straightening up.

"Mrs. Marsden, I need to see someone downstairs. I'll be back shortly. Maybe the time will give you an opportunity to gather your thoughts. Excuse me." He left the room.

"Grace, here's the coffee I brought back. Take one."

"Thanks Karen," I murmured. "I'd better *gather* my

thoughts like 'the Man' said." Karen rolled her eyes and smiled. She squeezed my hand across the table as I smiled and took a sip of the still hot coffee.

My mind drifted to the last time I had seen Ric Kramer. I remembered the look of pain in his eyes and I felt the same breath-choking lump in my throat. My hand tightened around the Styrofoam cup.

"Grace, is the coffee cold? You haven't taken another sip."

My brain fast-forwarded to the present. Karen stared at me waiting for some sign that I heard her. "Um, I guess I drifted. The coffee is fine." I took another sip of the now tepid liquid to assure her. I figured Ric would be back soon, but I really didn't have a statement. I mean, what did I see? What could I tell him? I had tied my yarn through my belt loop and now sat still except for the movement of my left hand worrying the material.

The door opened and Ric pushed through carrying a tray with three cups of coffee. "Here, Grace, I thought you might need this. I brought one for you too, Karen." Ric put down the tray and distributed the cups. He noticed the half empty one in front of me. I was ready to relive those few awful moments.

Instead of taking my statement, he walked over to the fireplace. A uniformed technician was taking pictures of the hole and area before moving the broken cement. Ric crouched down outside the taped area close to the tech's right shoulder. A short conversation ensued during which Ric turned on the balls of his feet to look up at me. He came back to the table. He glanced down at my busy hand.

"That must have been a shock. I'm sorry you had to see it. Are you okay?" His tone sounded gentle again. I nodded my head. I heard him say softly, "Gracie, go home."

"What about my statement?"

"Someone from my office will call you. They'll handle it. Just leave your number with the officer at the door. Good-bye, Grace." His voice sounded final.

Just then, Harry rushed through the door. His normally neatly combed blonde hair was wind blown over a crooked part. His blue eyes filled with relief when he saw me.

"Harry, what on earth—"

"I called him," Karen explained. "I didn't know if you should drive home."

I knew why Karen called. We all knew. In her mind, she did what she thought was right. In reality, her call and Harry's arrival only complicated matters. Harry reached my side in an instant.

"Darling, are you all right?" He held one of my hands between both of his. "Karen told me you discovered a body."

"A body. A person. In the fireplace. A skeleton. The hand, its bone." I stopped the disjointed answer. I felt queasy. I didn't know how I looked.

"Grace and I are finished. You can take her home." Ric's emphasis on home sounded loud in the nearly empty room.

"Finished with you? Well, yes, of course she is." Harry's sarcasm wasn't lost on anyone. "I thought Inspectors assigned detectives to investigate calls. Or did you grab this one when you suspected she might be here?"

This wasn't going well. I wanted to turn back the clock by one remark. My husband's parry was playing to Ric's advantage.

"We do respond when we're requested *personally*." Ric drew out the last word. He punctuated his answer with a dazzling smile. I saw the muscles in Harry's neck tighten. I knew he was fighting the urge to look at me. He wouldn't give

Ric the satisfaction of knowing that his remark had caught him off-guard.

To Karen and Ric, he presented a confident appearance, glossing over Ric's comment as though unimportant. I knew him. His answer was just a little too long in coming.

"Well of course. Karen would certainly think of calling you."

"That's right," Karen added too quickly. "Why else have a cop in the family?"

I turned to Harry. "I want to go home."

"Of course, darling." He put his arm around my shoulders and pulled me closer.

"Grace?" Ric's voice stopped me. Harry's arm tightened around me. I half turned and looked over his shoulder at Ric. Harry moved forward bringing me along. He opened the door, as I turned forward so as not to stumble. Ric's voice followed us out the door.

"I'll be in touch, Grace. Soon."

CHAPTER THREE

The ride home was too quiet. I wanted to tell Harry about the horrible discovery. I wanted to explain why I had asked for Ric. Instead, I leaned back, closed my eyes, and worked the material on my belt loop into a longer piece of macramé.

I figured Harry was bursting with questions, but it wasn't his style to badger me. He knew I'd talk to him once I sorted it out in my mind. He pulled the car into the garage, turned off the engine, and closed the overhead door. I felt him turn towards me. His touch was light on my shoulder. I opened my eyes and turned to face him.

"I don't understand myself why I asked for Ric. I—"

He interrupted my words with a slight squeeze on my shoulder. "Darling, come inside. You don't have to explain anything to me. You need to relax. Then if you want to talk, I'll be here."

Of course, he was right. I didn't do anything that needed an explanation. Once inside, I began to feel better about the whole situation. Harry suggested I take a hot bath. While I filled the tub, he offered to make me some tea. I really don't care for tea, but my English husband's answer to most crises was a hot soak and a hot cuppa. He never drank coffee, so we kept a well-stocked tea box in addition to several flavors of coffee beans for me. Karen always brought us enticing gifts of exotic sounding teas and beans from her travels abroad.

Hannah Marsden, Harry's twin sister, enclosed small packets of tea for her brother with most of her letters.

The room filled with the wonderful fragrance of jasmine from the scented cubes I crushed under the running water. I removed my clothing and pinned up my shoulder length hair while waiting impatiently for the water level to rise high enough to turn on the jets.

The shrill ring of the telephone startled me. I heard Harry's voice coming from downstairs. He answered so quickly he must have been standing next to the phone in the kitchen.

I set the timer for twenty minutes and carefully climbed into the inviting water. Perfect. Fragrant bubbles surrounded me. I slipped a terry cloth headband around my hairline. In spite of that precaution, errant wisps of dark hair escaped from beneath their restraints to curl up and plaster themselves against my neck and forehead.

The heat worked wonders on the muscles in my neck and shoulders, loosening them to the degree that I felt no stiffness. Leaning back against the bath cushion and stretching out full length brought a contented sigh from my soul. The water felt heavenly. I tried to empty my brain of the day's horror. My thoughts scampered back to the start of this day. The old cliché intruded on my thoughts. *If I knew then what I know now,* I would have stayed in bed and asked for a pass until the next day. It had been especially difficult leaving my warm bed and even warmer husband this morning. My thoughts gathered in *that* spot as I relived the day's beginning.

I executed a perfect half turn across warm, rumpled sheets into Harry Marsden's half open arms. The movement merited drowsy approval as he tightened his arms around me. *"The time is now seven o'clock. You've asked to be awakened at that hour. Enjoy your day."* Our innocuous timepiece was a wedding present from one of Harry's clients. It intoned three additional messages at five-minute intervals each became more demanding until its final message. That clarion was followed by a horrid buzzing sound that should be heard only in the North woods by wide-awake lumberjacks. Harry enjoyed the sticky sweet tones of the *woman* professing to have our best interests at heart. She was a ceramic figurine ala *Betty Boop*. He timed his departure from beneath the covers to the last possible moment; always chiding Betty for her lack of compassion.

I would gladly donate our bedside companion to the church bazaar except for Harry's insistence on the clock's originality. The only time I heard from *her* was the rare occasion when Harry lingered a nanosecond too long and the buzz-saw wake up call exploded into our peaceful morning. I was usually up and about when I'd hear a characteristic "bloody thing" as Harry lunged the last few feet to slap the molded, plastic derriere that turned off our strange bedfellow.

"Well, you've crashed into me, disrupted a beautiful dream, and now you're just lying there looking up at the ceiling." Harry released his grip on me and rolled over onto one elbow. His sapphire blue eyes were laughing, but his mouth pretended a sternness of which he was incapable. A thousand years could pass and I would never tire of gazing into his eyes. I pushed against Harry's arm. His weight shifted allowing me to put my arms around his muscular back. Not one to lose a moment he moved to hold me closer. An anticipatory sigh escaped my lips. Harry was just getting started. *"It is now 7:10. You requested to be awakened at 7:00. Enjoy your day."* Two more messages to go.

* * *

Subtle, soft music, barely discernible above the droning of the Jacuzzi, reached my ears. Harry must have popped one of my mood tapes into the player for me. I heard a clinking sound, like cup against saucer, as he placed my English *medicine* on the moss green terrazzo tiles surrounding the tub. I opened my eyes and turned my head toward the sound.

"Well, look at you. Your color is better already."

"It's the hot water that's turning me pink."

"That's right, old girl. A hot soak and a hot cuppa makes everything better."

"I know. I know. Is that adage on a needlepoint sampler in your home or is it on your ancestral coat of arms?"

He laughed and handed me my tea. Harry's laugh sounded pleasant and tender. "Go ahead, make fun of my heritage. We English know the value of hot water and warm whiskey." Pronouncement made he stood to leave.

"Who called earlier?"

"Oh," he hesitated, "the police called to confirm you're coming in tomorrow to make a statement. I told them we'd be there about ten o'clock."

"We?"

"Well, you don't think I'm going to let you go through that alone, do you?"

"What's to go through? I'll just give my statement and be out of there in ten minutes. And besides, what about the brunch you're supposed to attend tomorrow for the Society of Baker Street Regulars?"

"Damn, I'd forgotten about that. I'll just cancel. There will be plenty of literary types in attendance. They won't miss me."

"Harry, you promised Muriel you'd be there. This is the

third function of hers that you'll miss. Anyway, I'll be back home by noon. Tell you what. When I get back I'll marinate a couple of tenderloins and assemble a scrumptious Caesar's salad. You can make your traditional offering to the gods of the grill. We'll open a bottle of Gamy Beaujolais, and probably never make it back downstairs for dinner."

"Seems like a waste of a perfectly good dinner, but then we all know, 'man does not live by bread alone.'"

When Harry began quoting clichés, I knew I'd won the round. He left me to my soak. I leaned back against the cushion again and thought about my police statement. What *did* I see? A bead rolling out from a hole in the wall? A bony hand stretching down from the hole, as though trying to retrieve it? I took a few sips of the cinnamon spice flavored tea in an attempt to drive these thoughts from my mind.

Now questions replaced the awful thoughts. Who was the person? What happened? When did it happen? How did a body come to its final resting place behind a fireplace at my college? I rehashed those questions and others again and again until I felt the water cooling in the tub. Perhaps getting out and moving around would clear my thoughts. I dried off with an oversized bath towel embroidered with pink flamingos and slipped into a cranberry colored floor length wrapper. The pocket of the wrapper sported a tiny embroidered pink flamingo. I pushed my feet into shapeless pink ballet slippers.

The decor in the bath was tropical island with several avian touches. The walls teemed with pictures of flamingoes in different poses. The shelves and tile area held flamingo statues, flamingo cachepots, and even flamingo-shaped soaps. I was the flamingo freak. Harry sometimes balked at bathing with those *flamin' birds.*

I had decorated the living quarters. He had laid out the

rose garden and hedges. He was suspicious of my Italian heritage and drew the line at flamingos on the lawn. Harry also designed the library replicating a larger version he had visited in an English country home. Ours was a smaller scale but was exact even down to the sliding panel leading to the hidden priest's hole.

I realized I hadn't eaten since breakfast at Regina. A glance at the clock told me it was nearly 5:00 p.m. My stomach was urging me into the kitchen to check out the pantry. I passed Harry's office and heard the whirring of his printer. I knew that he would probably work for the next few hours and then emerge famished. Harry was a consummate *snacker.* He could skip substantial meals and survive on cheese, biscuits, tins of sardines, caviar, and smoked oysters. I had no idea why his cholesterol and blood pressure weren't sky-high. He attributed his health to an excellent metabolic rate and a moderate English appetite. I think in all the years I have known him he has eaten maybe two cheeseburgers. I survived college on macaroni and cheese, peanut butter and jelly sandwiches, and McDonald's.

Pulling things from the refrigerator and pantry shelves, I had my ham and Swiss on rye assembled when my attention wandered to the small TV in the kitchen. Maybe Regina College would be on the news. I turned on the set. The announcer gave the lead-in for his next story before he broke away for station identification.

"Harry. Harry, come here. Hurry." He rushed into the kitchen just as the evening news resumed.

"Grace, what's wrong?"

"Regina made the evening news." I pointed to the TV. His eyes followed my direction.

"A bizarre discovery at Regina College in River Forest

tops our evening news. A skeleton was discovered behind a wall in the college library. The police investigation, headed by Inspector Ric Kramer, is ongoing this evening at the campus. The police are not offering any comment at this time. Alumna Grace Marsden made the actual discovery."

My heart pounded as the screen filled with two photographs. One was of me, a faculty yearbook photo, and next to that, one of a younger Ric Kramer taken when he was still a detective.

I felt frozen to the spot. The announcer's voice continued.

"Besides the horror of the discovery there is a note of irony in this situation. Some of you may remember that Grace Marsden and Inspector Ric Kramer made headlines during a homicide investigation seven years ago when Inspector Kramer solved the murder of an influential businessman. That murder case was connected to the disappearance of Mrs. Marsden's husband, well-known publisher Harry Marsden and Derek Rhodes, an associate with the publishing firm. We will have more details on the fireplace skeleton story as they become available."

The blood ran cold in my veins. My arms and legs felt weighted down. I was stunned that this unhappy part of our past had been so carelessly exposed to a new group of viewers. I thought the days of seeing myself and hearing my life on the evening news were behind me. Harry's astonished look slowly turned to one of rage.

"Bloody fools! Damn idiots! They haven't any details so they dredge up that story. I'm calling that station manager. Damn him. What gives him the right to air that piece?" The vein on the side of his neck stood out, throbbing with the hot blood coursing through it.

"Harry please, don't do this to yourself. Those stories are

in the public domain. You know that. We can't stop them."
He seemed to calm down a bit. His anger was still apparent in
the slight trembling of his right hand. That nervous habit
began after his incarceration in a South American prison.
When he came home, he suffered from involuntary spasms.
His doctor said they were a manifestation of the abuse he
suffered in prison; although Harry's strong mind had remained
intact, his body had capitulated to the torturous rigors of
imprisonment. The trauma caused a slight stroke that left him
with a weakened right side. Eighteen months of painful
therapy and exercise had returned Harry to his previous vigor
and mobility with the exception of an almost imperceptible
limp.

"Grace, I won't have you put through this again. I won't
allow them to hurt you." The phone rang before I could
respond. We both stared at the instrument as though it were
alive with a mind of its own. I was certain the call was a
reporter looking for a usable quote. Then, in a moment, relief
replaced my fear. We recently had installed caller ID and a
quick glance at the display window told me it was Karen's
number. I grabbed the receiver on the third ring.

"Karen?" I asked breathlessly.

"No, Grace, it's Ric." My throat tightened. I knew he'd
seen the broadcast. Why was he calling?

"Grace, did you see the..."

"Yes, we just saw it," I interrupted.

"I want you to know that I didn't comment about anything
that happened before. In fact, I just hung up with the station
manager who gave me his word that he wouldn't run that story
with this current investigation. Uncle Richard had just finished
his own call to him. I want you to know that."

I was silent, thinking about Ric's uncle and how helpful

he'd been in securing Harry's release.

"Grace, are you there?" Ric asked.

"Ah, yes, I'm sorry. I'm listening."

"I also want to warn you not to come down to the station tomorrow. I know you're supposed to be here at ten o'clock, but I'm afraid there might be some nosy reporters hanging around."

"What should I do about my statement?" Now the silence was on Ric's part. "Ric?"

"Grace, I'll come out there tomorrow morning, take your statement and be done with it." He rushed to explain, "I don't want some officer leaking information to the press or trying to dig up anything from before. I'll be there at ten-thirty." Ric hung up before I could say no.

"He's coming out here tomorrow, isn't he?" Harry asked. I repeated the conversation, almost verbatim, to Harry. His response was expected.

"How nice for you. The inspector is still exerting his family's influence on your behalf. Still watching over you as it were."

"Harry that's not fair. I didn't ask him to do this for me. I barely spoke to him."

"But Grace, that is what is so endearing about a lady in distress." Harry's sarcasm was hurtful. I had felt the barbs of his angry words when he first found out what happened between Ric and me while he was in prison. Through the years, he had begun to understand and to forgive, but he had never been able to forget that his young wife had fallen in love with the person who became the instrument of his rescue. Painful feelings I thought behind us, had in one day, surfaced again to hurt us.

I turned my head away from him, more to hide my tears

then to stop the argument I knew would follow. There were no more harsh words. I turned to look at Harry. He was leaning forward with his head down. His hands clenched the counter's edge. From the depths of his soul, I heard a quiet voice. "I'm sorry, Grace. Please forgive me." He sounded so hurt. I moved to put my arms around his shoulders.

"Please don't. I love you. We can't let this hurt us again."

"I'm so sorry" he repeated.

"This hasn't been easy on either of us." He lifted his head and looked into my eyes. His eyes were moist; mine were streaming with tears.

"I'm just feeling inadequate, Love. I wanted to rave at that station manager and make him stop. I wanted to be the one to protect you. Instead of being grateful that the job got done, I was jealous that Kramer did it."

"I know, Darling," I soothed. "But you do protect me, and love me, and thrill me and laugh with me and all the other things that make us special. It doesn't matter who flexed whose muscle, does it?"

"I'm just jealous I suppose. A husband, after all, wants to be his wife's hero."

"Don't be jealous," I stopped him. "Heroes are occasional, but soul mates are forever." Harry embraced me tenderly.

"How was I so lucky to find you?"

I tilted my face toward his. "Ditto." He kissed me gently. I felt the imprint of his lips after he pulled away from my willing mouth. For the second time that day I gazed into his eyes. At times, they were exactly as I remembered them from the spring day so many years ago, before the uncertainty and pain of our early life together.

CHAPTER FOUR

Spring 1982

The College was hosting a champagne brunch Sunday afternoon to make note of another feather in its' academic cap. Dan Carlton, a professor in the speech department, had just published in his field. Regina College relished any occasion to honor one of their own. Since the doors had opened in 1922, accepting the daughters of well to do Irish and Italian Catholic families, Regina held Sunday afternoon brunches to celebrate events. Sister Claire, Dean of the college, offered the welcoming speech precisely at Noon. Her delightfully few lines were followed by the perfunctory speeches of Sister Lawrence, President of the college, Dr. Roland Magnus, head of the Speech department and finally, Professor Daniel Carlton. Professor Carlton was charming, modest, and adamant in his insistence that the college family of faculty and student body inspired his efforts.

With praise and kudos behind us, we escaped from the small recital hall to the quadrangle and cloister walk, the prettiest place on campus. Parents, first seeing this view of the college, immediately signed on the dotted line for their precious offspring. The quadrangle was a beautifully manicured expanse of lawn rolling gently toward the circular drive that was the main access to Regina. This perfect green was bordered on three sides by appropriately gothic architecture, and just the right amount of hardy English Ivy clinging to hallowed halls. The covered portico that connected Lewis and Power Halls was known as the cloister walk. The imagery was a subtle mix of higher education, finishing school, and convent.

Today, several round tables had been set up on the lawn. Each table was covered with fresh white linen embroidered at the hem with cut linen roses. The stiff breeze blowing from the North was doing its best to force the edges up onto the tabletops. Although it was only the end of April, the weather had cooperated with the college's outdoor affair. A spiritual quid pro quo between all those nuns and the heavens above was always a popular explanation. The day was mild and the sky a cornflower blue, with a scattering of cotton puff clouds. Perfect for a Sunday brunch.

The college had always employed students to serve at various functions. Young ladies from the college, appropriately mannered and attired, carried trays of gleaming silver among the guests; each tray holding fluted glasses filled to the proper level with champagne. Each delicate flute sparkled in the bright sunlight, like a small prism catching and scattering the sun in a burst of color.

Professor Carlton was positioned at a central table that held a display of his new book. He signed the end page with a flourish as he chatted graciously with each patron. My classmates and I skirted his table, as we hadn't the desire to purchase his book. We had a collective eye on the long tables beckoning from under the cloister walk. Both tables held heavy sterling chaffing dishes, each filled with a different delight. Drinks in hand, we moved to investigate.

One dish held hundreds of tiny meatballs simmering in a wine-laced sauce. The next two chafing dishes brimmed with lobster thermidor. The guests were already standing two-deep at those. The last hot hors d'oeuvre was rumaki. Placed between the chafing dishes were trays of finger sandwiches, thin cucumber slices spread with anchovy butter on small points of toast and cream cheese with slivers of pimiento on cocktail rye. In addition to the sandwiches, the guests were treated to a cut crystal bowl filled with caviar. Smaller crystal bowls holding lemons, sour cream and toasted triangles formed a front line for the assault that was sure to follow.

I remembered a movie with Grace Kelly dining 'al fresco.' She allowed herself only a few goodies on her plate. Reminded of her poise and fabulous figure, I turned away from the feast long before my friends completed their choices. At five feet, four inches tall and 106 pounds I wasn't too concerned about my figure. I hoped my Irish genes would keep me lean, but I knew my pasta genes were out there lurking.

I had moved away from the buffet when I realized that I had carelessly left my champagne glass between the rumaki and the cucumber sandwiches. It seemed easier to secure another rather than shoulder through to the front, so I looked for the flash of sterling silver.

"Might this be what you're looking for?" He was definitely attractive, but not to distraction. In the few seconds that everyone takes to make a snap decision, I made mine. His expressive deep blue eyes could probably either glint or gleam depending on his mood. The Saville Row suit, in soft shades of deep blue fit him beautifully. His six-foot frame filled it admirably. His absolutely dazzling smile interested me the most during this three-second survey.

"It was thoughtful of you to notice I'd left it behind." I accepted my glass and thanked him.

"I would have introduced myself to you before too long.

At least now, I'm not empty-handed. Harry Marsden." He extended his hand. That smile again! His handshake was firm and lingered a moment. His hands suited his appearance. Sometimes people's hands don't look like the rest of them, but his did. They felt firm, not fleshy and soft like a sedentary executive, but not callused.

"I'm Professor Carlton's publisher. Actually, we've quite a few authors from Regina College." The accent was more apparent after a few sentences. Definitely English and, if my ear remembered the voices from my junior year exchange program, probably London. Suddenly, I realized that he had finished his introduction and was looking at me rather expectantly.

"How do you do. I'm Grace Morelli, one of Professor Carlton's students. Several of us thought we'd come along to add our voices to the crowd." His smile seemed to waiver when I told him I was a student. I looked past his left ear at a motion behind him and instantly regretted the lapse in eye contact. He turned and spotted my friends waving at me from one of the tables.

"It seems your friends are holding a place for you. I won't keep you. Nice to have met you, Miss Morelli," he said as he offered his hand again.

"Nice to have met you, Mr. Marsden. I hope you enjoy your afternoon at Regina."

"I already have." His smile flashed up to his eyes. I was right; they could gleam! He turned and walked toward a table near Professor Carlton. A very blonde and strikingly beautiful woman half turned and smiled at Harry Marsden when he touched her shoulder as he moved round her to take his seat. Her eyes were a stunning shade of turquoise and her gaze followed him in a proprietary manner. *What a dolt I am! Of course he wouldn't be here alone.* I joined my friends, who by this time had stopped waving and were now engaged in devouring their food. I was intent on explaining a sudden and strange knot in the pit of my stomach. I pushed some food about my plate with my fork until Karen offered to take the untouched hors d'oeuvres off my hands. In between mouthfuls, she wanted the story on the great looking man she'd seen me talking to and why on earth hadn't I brought him over to give all of them a closer look.

"He's not on display Karen, for goodness sake." I spoke a little too sharply. Three pairs of eyes, two brown, one blue, fixed on me with a questioning look. "Anyway, he's with an incredibly beautiful person." I made that statement and turned my head to glance at his table as if to confirm my facts. He was gone. So was the blonde. He had fulfilled his obligation to appear and had left as quickly as was proper. I felt a pang of disappointment that he'd gone.

"Are you thinking of those early days, Gracie?" Harry's voice brought me back to the nineties. My startled expression told him he was right.

"I think your ancestors must be part Druid. It's eerie the way you read my thoughts."

"Let's go home for the summer solstice and I'll introduce you to a few... ancestors that is."

Home to Harry would always be Arundel, a beautiful, charming village along the southern coast of England. Although Harry had lived in the United States for twenty years and here in Chicago for the last thirteen, he never missed an opportunity to get back home to friends, family and a past that held no darkness or sadness. After trips home to his roots, he always returned refreshed, somehow more youthful in his demeanor. Nothing could erase or soften the expression of sadness that lived in his eyes and around his mouth. Subtle, but permanent changes that marked him.

My friends think he looks very sexy and James Bondish, the Roger Moore version as Harry is blond and blue-eyed. Only a few close friends know that he actually did live through a Bond script. One gone terribly wrong.

CHAPTER FIVE

Harry grumbled about going to this soiree. It was nine a.m. He had stalled over tea and a muffin and changed his shirt twice. Muriel Faye had a fine reputation in the industry and Harry wanted to support her efforts. The brunch sounded lovely and although I could have accompanied him, I had the distinct feeling the one time I did attend that most of these matronly types would be much happier with my absence. Harry was very handsome and so-o-o charming and so-o-o English. His parting words were to remind me to go easy on the anchovies in the Caesar's salad.

I knew he was uncomfortable about Ric Kramer coming here this morning. I touched his cheek as he left. "I love you," I assured him.

"I know." He smiled.

An hour and a half later I opened the door for Ric. He arrived a few minutes early, but I had been ready since nine a.m. Our first few comments were strained. I offered him coffee as we sat down in the living room. He assumed his police role and after a brief question and answer period, Ric closed his notepad saying that a statement would be typed up for me to sign. He stood to leave.

"More coffee?" I asked.

"Sure, I've time for one more cup." He looked at his watch as though to confirm his statement. Ric seemed to relax a little as he settled back in his chair. I probably shouldn't have prolonged our meeting but I was curious about the skeleton. I hoped Rick didn't think there was more than just coffee on the table.

"Have you learned anything about—it?"

An expression of annoyance passed across his face and he sat up straighter before he answered. "We don't have an official report from the forensic lab. That will take another day or so. One of our guys is working on his thesis in forensic osteology so he tinkered around with the remains and did some measurements of the skull and long bones. He figures that the skeleton was a female, about five feet, four inches tall, slight to medium in stature, and in her early twenties at the time of death. She's been in that wall for probably fifty years. She was wearing some sort of a fancy dress; we found bits of lace and some beads, most of the other beads were probably carried off by rats—"

"Oh," coffee sloshed in the mug as I put it down abruptly.

"I'm sorry, stupid of me," Ric apologized.

"No, it's okay I asked for it."

Ric's recitation of his report in such an official tone didn't deal with the sadness of the death of someone so young. "How awful! Who could have killed someone that way?"

"Hold on Gracie...uh, Grace. The coroner says a hard blow to the head was the cause of death. Her skull was cracked here." Ric lifted a hand and touched the left side of his head. "Most likely, she was already dead when someone sealed her inside that wall."

"It's still awful. Any idea who she was?"

"We've done some routine background checks. We checked with the college's records of when the fireplace was installed. The company that did the build out of the library was sloppy when it came to record keeping. We know the library was completed and dedicated in early December 1941. We have some information on contractors that bid on various aspects of the project, but no actual billings to determine who got the contracts. Five companies bid on the masonry work alone. Three companies bid on the stone carving job for the mantelpiece. Having a time line made it easy to check on records of missing persons. No one had reported anyone fitting this description missing. We've taken the inquiry as far back as we could. I doubt that we'll assign any more manpower to a fifty year old crime."

"You mean you're not going to try and find out anything? What if her family has been wondering about her all these years? Don't they deserve to know what happened? What about the fact that there is no statute of limitations on murder?"

"Grace, it's a dead end. We're talking fifty years ago. We don't even know if she had family. We have no place to start." Ric stood up and ran his hand over his thick black hair. He walked toward the Baldwin piano in the corner.

"Hey, you still play this antique?" He smiled brightly for a moment and then seemed to remember himself. "Grace, it's useless. We're closing the books on it once we get all the paperwork filed. Homicide by *party or parties unknown*," he chanted.

"The least you could do is try to find out who she was. It would be some kind of release for her family after all this time. She probably went to Regina since she was...ah, there, you know.

"Grace, why are you so wrapped up in this?"

"Because I know what it's like to wonder. If they're alive, if they're okay, if you'll ever see them again." My voice trembled. "I know that agony first hand. But more than that, I know what it's like for a family to watch someone they love pine for their missing loved one year after year until part of them goes missing too. You know my mother's older sister disappeared during the war. My mom never could accept that loss, that lack of closure. I can't help wondering..." my voice quivered then stopped.

"Grace, come on. You can't possible think this skeleton is your Aunt. Don't be silly. You're the one who showed me the letter she mailed home fifty years ago. You told me that the family believed she'd left school to avoid marriage. That she'd jilted some poor sucker."

"I know what I told you, but what if she didn't run off? My mother never really believed it. The college had mailed my aunt's diary to my mother and great aunt. That's all the college sent. Aunt Fiona believed the letter was true because Cecilia's trunk was never sent and because Aunt Fiona always seemed to want to believe the worst of people. Mother knew her sister would never leave her diary behind, it was always under her pillow. What about DNA tests? Wouldn't they show something?"

"Grace, I can't just order DNA tests on a whim. There's no probable connection to justify spending the taxpayers' dollars on your personal mission. I'm sorry."

"Well aren't there files we could look at, maybe people we could talk to..."

We?" Ric asked. "Are you really suggesting *we* look into this together?"

"It's a figure of speech, Ric."

"No," he countered, "it's a pronoun meaning, in this case, you and me."

"Ric, it's been years since we were together. It's been years since we've even spoken to each other. Let's just leave it at that. Now we're at least talking to each other. We have our own lives. I mean, I know you've been working hard..."

"Gracie, you're braiding. You always braid when you're nervous." Ric gestured toward my hands, which were furiously twisting and looping a piece of yellow yarn that had been forgotten on the coffee table until my nervous fingers had snatched it up.

"And you don't know how hard I've been working. You don't know that I've worked that hard, that long, to keep thoughts of you out of my mind. First, you couldn't leave Harry because he was so sick when he came home. Then you said you couldn't tell him about us because he was *psychologically vulnerable*. Then little by little you stopped calling, stopped visiting Karen, stopped returning my calls, and finally, the long vacation in England to help Harry regain his strength." Ric stopped talking and started pacing. He moved near the piano again. "You know, it's ironic, Grace. Harry told you that constantly thinking about you was what kept him from going crazy. Thinking about you was what almost drove me crazy!" His slow, enigmatic smile made me shiver. I felt chilled in spite of the flush his comments were prompting.

"Ric, this isn't fair. I told you how things happened when we were in England. Harry and I had time together to discover feelings about each other. I told him about us not because I wanted to leave, but because I wanted to stay."

"Yeah, I know. You told me. I wonder if you could imagine how many times I've wished for a different ending."

"Ric please, don't."

"I'd better be leaving. Sorry if you think River Forest's finest isn't doing the job, but there really is nothing to follow. We have current cases to work on." Ric crossed the room to where I was standing. He cupped my chin in his hand and tilted up my face.

"I can't be around you Gracie. It still hurts." He lowered his hand to his side, turned, and walked out the door.

During the last few minutes of our conversation, I had the uneasy feeling that we were being watched through the French doors. I was certain there had been a shadow, pulling back quickly, when I turned toward the kitchen. Nothing but sunshine now.

The time with Ric stressed me more than I realized. I felt dazed and tired with a churning sensation in the pit of my stomach. I decided to try my second favorite method of unwinding (pity that my most favorite was at a brunch) and take April, my Tennessee Walker, for a long ride. I know April isn't a hotshot name for a horse, but she's not a hotshot horse.

I had met April Showers, an unsuccessful show horse with a choppy gait and a desperate need for a friend, about eight years ago. She was doomed to be sold to a petting zoo or something equally degrading because her performance was not show quality. She had a heart that wanted to please and a sweet disposition with everyone, especially children. My niece and nephews all learned to ride on my gentle reject. I didn't mind her imperfect gait. I knew I didn't sit a horse as splendidly as her previous owner.

I had met her owners, Susan and Preston Greene, at a Special Olympics Event that Karen and I co-chaired. I thought Susan and I could become good friends, and Harry seemed to enjoy Preston's company. They went riding and golfing together several times in the months after we met. Susan and I were planning a trip to Galena. A friend of mine had renovated a beautiful old mansion on the Mississippi's bluffs into a charming bed and breakfast. She named it Mississippi Martha.

I had seen the drawings and then the early stages of remodeling. Martha's grand opening was in three weeks and I had some knickknacks I had offered her for her B&B. Our plans were set and I suggested that we invite Karen for the weekend. Susan's reaction prompted the end of our neophyte relationship. She objected strongly to including Karen in anything we did.

"I can't imagine how you can be friends with someone who has chosen to live her life so differently than we do." Her voice lowered to include me in her confidence as she continued. "I know this is the nineties and everyone's come out of the closet, but I personally don't know what to say to her. Preston and I really enjoy you and Harry, but it's such a strain on us knowing that Karen is so close to both of you."

Her smug, self-righteous attitude sickened me. She began a *whispering campaign* against including Karen on the steering committee of a new literacy program. That was until Aunt Shelly heard about it. Karen's protective aunt mounted a counterattack and she didn't whisper. Susan soon missed invitations to several outings and committees. Aunt Shelly never forgave or forgot a perceived affront to her family name. Afterward, I found out from a groom at Susan's stable that she was planning on having April destroyed if she couldn't unload her. Negotiations were handled through Preston and Harry.

Now, when Susan and I occasionally see each other at functions she waggles her fingers at me and smiles like we're old chums. I guess an 'across the room' friendship with me doesn't strain her too much.

I hoped a turf-pounding ride would chase memories of Ric from my brain, so I changed into riding clothes and saddled April. Unfortunately, the webs I had spun years ago wouldn't blow from my mind like so much gossamer on a windy day. I would never be able to forget what had happened seven years ago between Ric and me. So much of my today was a direct result of Ric.

When I desperately needed help in finding the truth about Harry's disappearance Karen just happened to have a brother who was a police detective. I remembered her brother Ric. I had seen him several times at Karen's house when we were younger. He was always gorgeous and worth staring at. He had served in Viet Nam for most of our college years, but I remembered attending his homecoming party. I had been reluctant to ask for help from the local authorities. They had all but patted me on the head and told me I should check again with Harry's friends and family. Sometimes 'husbands take time to work through things' they had said.

Karen insisted that Ric would listen and that he had connections, mainly their Uncle Richard, a retired Senator. I was desperate and Ric seemed competent. When I first told him the story of Harry's disappearance he had listened very carefully, writing notes on a pad but always looking into my eyes to reassure me. He had asked what I thought had been intelligent questions about Harry's habits and his friends and associates. We talked to everyone who had any contact with Harry before his disappearance from the convention he was attending in Rio de Janeiro. He had asked personal questions too. I had answered honestly. Maybe, too honestly.

Without my guidance, April picked her way to a favorite hillock at the back of Pine Marsh. Tall grass grew sweet and plentiful and the view of Pine Lake reflected serenity. A perfect spot. Thoughts of Ric and all we once were clung to me. The crisp breeze across the late autumn-chilled water touched my face, drying the tears meekly slipping down my cheeks. April pawed at a tuft of clover and startled me out of my reverie. Harry would be back soon. I turned us toward home. A low 'giddy up' and a shift in leg pressure signaled April to stretch out to a smooth gallop. The thud of her hooves on the carpet of grass matched the pounding of my heart against my rib cage. We swept by stirrup-high purple thistle, black-eyed susans, and clumps of wild daisies. Clods of dirt flew behind us marking our trail. We slowed to a choppy trot, then a lopsided walk and crossed the wooden bridge spanning the marsh. When I led April around the far side of the barn, I saw Ric sitting on the patio. What on earth? I'd been riding for over an hour. He waved and walked toward me. Ric had never ridden until he met April, another one of her conquests. He picked up a brush and began to brush her the way I had taught him.

"Well," I said expectantly.

"Well, what?"

"Well, you left over an hour ago. Why are you here? You made it quite plain that you were finished."

"That's why I came back, Grace. I don't know if I can ever be finished with you." His eyes were soft and tender. I made a conscious effort to look away. I pulled on April's lead harder then necessary and walked her into her box. I slipped her a few baby carrots as an apology for my lapse in manners. We walked back to the patio in silence. More for something to do than for any other reason, I began the cumbersome task of removing my riding boots.

"Wait, I remember that too." Ric stood, mounted my leg and presented me with his backside in the time honored posture of valet to master. "Madam?" his deep voice intoned as he gripped my thigh between his legs. I giggled at the thought of the boot print I was about to make on the backside of his Armani. He must have deciphered my giggle because at that instant he reached behind and grabbed my free boot thereby rendering me immobile and on the verge of being pulled off the bench onto my jodhpured bottom.

In the next instant, Harry strolled around the corner and stopped dead in his tracks. He recoiled a little, as though he had smacked up against an invisible wall. His smile slipped silently from his lips. One eyebrow arched over a frosty blue eye demanded an explanation.

In the ensuing rush to disengage ourselves, we looked like Laurel and Hardy. I almost did land on my rear as Ric tried to step forward. He hadn't let go of my foot and couldn't swing his leg over mine without tangling us more. It was probably only fifteen seconds, but it seemed like five minutes. Then I noticed Harry's face. The anger I expected to see wasn't there. A minuscule smile poked at a corner of his mouth.

"Hello Kramer. Interesting techniques you American chaps have while investigating a crime." Harry's smooth-as-silk voice didn't fool me. When he put on the 'Brit' he was hiding something. An equally smooth brow accompanied his barb. I knew mine was furrowed like a row of corn in an Iowa field. Ric must have been just as confused at Harry's lack of reaction. He was speechless. At long last Ric answered, "Cut the crap Marsden, I'm just helping..."

"Yourself to my wife," Harry finished.

"No dammit. What you saw was..."

"Oh, I do understand exactly what I saw," Harry interrupted again.

"Harry, stop it!" I found my own truant voice. "It's not what you think. I'm not even sure what you think, but if it's not what it is then that's not it!" I sputtered in my best Laura Petrie logic.

In spite or maybe because of the situation we laughed.

Harry draped his arm around me in a very proprietary manner and waved off Ric with his other hand saying, "We'll call when we need your services, Jeeves!" A second barb reducing Ric's role to that of a gentleman's gentleman. A peek past Harry's left ear showed me a pissed off Inspector. Ten minutes ago, I would have bet the outcome much differently.

CHAPTER SIX

That afternoon, I repeated Ric's comments about the investigation to Harry, careful to leave out other details. After all, you could press a person's buttons only so many times before you elicited a response you might regret.

I decided to edit some galleys before we grilled our dinner. Harry left to putter in his rose garden. Instead of editing, I began thinking of ways to track this unknown woman. If the police weren't going to pursue the investigation, that didn't mean I couldn't. I felt I had to try. For my mother.

My years as a librarian and my natural penchant for solving puzzles provided me with many contacts and several proven methods. I began by listing available records from that era. There would be accounts of construction or renovation in the school files. I knew my search would be more thorough than the cursory check the police made. Ric said they thought the body had been there for fifty years, since the dedication. That information would at least narrow my search quite a bit. Checking Regina's records was first on my list. I knew several people at the college who could help me. I even knew a few nuns who were old enough to have been at Regina fifty years ago.

Sister Andrew had taught English Literature at Regina and her name leaped to the top of my mental list. Anyone who had majored in English in the last forty years probably had several courses with Sister Andrew, including me. Everyone loved her. She was one of those people who always kept an open mind to new trends, even ones she wasn't fond of. She didn't just tolerate or suffer through younger ideas and newer methods, she really gave our music, hair styles, and clothes a fair chance. We called her Sister A because it was the seventies and we thought she was *cool*. She was more than a teacher to me; she had been my student advisor during my senior year. More than anyone else at that time in my life, she believed in me. She also encouraged me to write my first children's book and then encouraged me to write the second and the third until finally I found a publisher who thought "Mick the Monster" might actually sell. I dialed the number I knew by heart and left a message at the college switchboard asking her to call. After Regina contacts, the newspaper archives would be my second stop. If anything odd or unusual had happened at the school, the local paper, Forest News, which had been publishing River Forest doings for over seventy years, would have a write up.

Harry entered the room from the patio, balancing his teacup, *Tribune*, and one perfect rose. A small flourish and loving smile accompanied, "Here darling, my first Grace." Harry's passion for roses surely developed from his English genes. His garden boasted several prize-winning varieties. Harry's first attempt at typical English cottage flowers didn't fare too well in our Chicago climate, but the heartier species like English Lavender, Primrose, and Canterbury Bells continued to do well. His roses, however, were beautiful and prolific bloomers. He devoted hours to his garden and even found time to exhibit at shows. One of the largest shows of the year, at the Botanical Gardens, would feature his newest success, 'Grace.' I accepted the rose and reached up to kiss him. "Harry, it's beautiful. I love having a rose named after me. It's so romantic."

"That's me darling, Mr. Romance. And I am not going to let anything spoil this moment, not even that thorn-in-the-side Inspector." We both laughed as he folded his arms around me. The rose was a deep violet color tinged with cream on the edges of the petals. I carefully placed the flower in a Capodimonte vase that had belonged to my mother. The vase didn't really match our contemporary decor, but it was a remembrance of her and therefore had a special spot in the house.

"It's still not a perfect match to your eyes, but then nothing is." My otherwise dark Mediterranean heritage was tempered by my mother's Irish origins. Thick, wavy, sable brown hair was undoubtedly my father's input. The lighter complexion and the pansy violet eyes were definitely the results of some unusual genetic coupling.

I had been named after Grace Kelly, my dad's favorite movie star. The family choices had been Mary Eileen on my mom's side or Rosemary on my dad's side. At the eleventh hour, my dad decided to break with tradition and I was baptized Grace Eileen. He got his movie star name, but told my nana that Grace was American for Gracianna. My mom told her aunt that the middle name Eileen represented my Irish blood. My mother had wanted to name me after her older sister who had disappeared long before I was born, but my father had bad feelings about that. My misrepresented moniker led to nicknames of Gracie, Gem (initials from Grace Eileen Morelli), and now a rose named 'Grace.'

"It's beautiful," I assured Harry. "You'll win with this one."

"I already have," he murmured holding me close.

The phone rang at that moment, interrupting a mood that was leading to the bedroom. Instead of romance, we were grabbing our jackets and dashing for the car.

Forty-five minutes later Sister Andrew met us at the door to Power Hall. Her dimpled smile widened as I reached her side and bent down to hug her. I'm not tall but Sister was only four feet, eleven inches. She always seemed taller in class when you hadn't studied your Chaucer and she called on you. Her bright, blue eyes would flash as she 'caught' you, but her quick smile would encourage you to be ready next time.

Her eyes still shone bright with good humor and sharp wit. White hair, peeking from beneath her veil, framed her amazingly unlined face. Sister Andrew had chosen to keep wearing her long, white Dominican habit, even after 'street clothes' were approved by the order.

We followed her spry step down the corridor to one of the 'fishbowls'. So named because the rooms had doors for privacy of speech, but no curtains or blinds covered the glass door or the large windows facing the hallway. In earlier days at the college a young lady could sit and visit with her gentleman caller in these rooms. After all, how much privacy did a good Catholic girl need?

She offered us tea and made small talk until she had poured and we were settled. When she had returned my call earlier, I had explained my idea about tracking the identity of the skeleton. Sister said a visit with me was always welcome, but she didn't think she could help.

"Now remember, I had just arrived at Regina in the fall of forty-one," she started. "I had been given a camera, one of those new Brownies, and a set of blank journals to record my new life as a teacher. The books were a set of twelve with a beautiful, different cover on each one. The colors were the jewel tones I think they call them. You know, dear, the turquoise, and amethyst and sapphire colors."

I nodded that I knew the colors. "The newspaper said that the skeleton must have been in the wall for at least fifty years. Have you been keeping a journal for that long?"

"Oh, goodness yes. At least that long. It's a habit I began at college. Keeping a journal was very fashionable during the 1930's. Many immigrants kept journals as a way of recording everyday events to send news to their loved ones back home. Some of us, away from home for the first time, used daily journals as a way to *talk* to our families. Anyway, recollections of those days would be in my first journal since the old library was dedicated on Pearl Harbor Day. I'll never forget that day."

"Sister, that's wonderful. May we look at the journal?"

"Well of course. Well, actually I don't have it here. Perhaps you could help me find it."

"Find it?" interrupted Harry. "Excuse me Sister Andrew, but haven't you got it?"

"I do and I don't. She raised the teapot in an offer of refills. We both shook our heads no. Oh dear, I should explain."

Sister Andrew was adorable, but now in her late seventies, she seemed a little foggy on details. "You see Grace, several years ago when we Sisters moved from the old quarters, I needed to box up many of my books and papers as there wasn't enough space in my room. Well, Don Martin, the nice handyman, brought me a large trunk for my things. He said it had been in storage along with others for years, as long as he could remember. He got the idea to put these old trunks to use and get them out of the way. Over the next few years, we filled all the trunks.

The first one he brought me had some very old clothes and some tea things. I donated the clothes to the drama department for their wardrobe. I kept the china. In fact, we're using it now. Isn't it lovely? I always liked the tiny floral pattern. Irish, I think."

"I think you're right Sister," agreed Harry, "but you were saying about the trunk?"

Sister Andrew beamed at Harry. "Oh yes. Well, I put all my journals and books inside. Mr. Martin was kind enough to remove the trunk to storage."

"That's great. Where is it now, and we'll make arrangements to pick it up?"

"Oh, well, you see I'm not sure. A few years after Mr. Martin moved my trunk, he fell and broke his hip. The bone never mended properly so he had to take disability. That was fifteen or so years ago."

Sister Andrew suddenly seemed aware of how dim the chances were of finding Mr. Martin or her trunks. She smiled weakly and offered more tea. "Oh dear, it was so long ago and my memory doesn't always keep things in order. I'm going to sit here with my tea, child, and try to think back to that time."

I hugged Sister Andrew again and promised to let her know if we turned up any trunks. On our way out of the college, we stopped in the secretary's office to see Betty Dulaney and ask about old employment records. I explained that we were trying to trace Mr. Martin. Betty disputed Sister's timeframe. She told us that Don Martin had left the college about two years before Betty started and she was celebrating twenty-one years of employment in April. Betty thought those records were on fiche and she promised to take a look the first chance she had time. I thanked her and left my number. The trail seemed to have evaporated. I remembered Ric's words 'dead end' and began feeling some misgivings about my ability to discover anything.

We retraced our steps for a final good-bye. Sister Andrew looked deep in thought of days long ago. She had a sweet, studied expression on her face. Harry motioned me away from the door and I turned, wondering if Sister A had recaptured December 1941.

Sister Andrew's talk of journals reminded me that I had access to an excellent account of the time in question through my aunt's own diary. It had been returned to my mother after Aunt Cecilia disappeared. "Harry, let's go by my dad's house. I want to look for my aunt's diary."

"No problem. Only let's stop in and not just *go by*. Seems a shame not to pop in and say hello to your dad."

"Oh shush," I interrupted. "That's not what I meant." Harry never missed an opportunity to point out the language idiosyncrasies of Americans in general and Midwesterners in particular. "I know my dad has all of my mother's things packed in boxes in the attic. He's been meaning to go through them and all. Maybe this will help him get around to it."

The ride to my dad's house was short and direct via the Eisenhower Expressway. We exited at Wolf Road and took that north to Bohlander Avenue reaching the corner of Victoria and Bohlander in no time. The brick bungalow looked sturdy and inviting. My dad took a week each summer and gathered his sons and daughter. We scraped, painted, fixed, mended, replaced, and built whatever needed doing. What the Morellis and friends couldn't do, my dad hired out. Over the years, he hadn't hired much.

Dad would cook up a *taste of Italia* for the volunteers. He would prepare ravioli with pesto, three cheese baked lasagna, meatballs in marinara gravy, tasty bruschetta and thick homemade pizza. Mom would fuss with serving and cleanup. She'd also baby-sit her cherished grand kids while their parents toiled away on the homestead.

I had invited Karen the first summer I met her. She loved the food. She loved the company even more. With the exception of her brief and disastrous marriage one summer, she hadn't missed the event in over ten years. It was a treat to be invited to the summer cleanup and pig-out at the Morelli home. With my mother gone, it wasn't the same, but the tradition continued. Some of her grand kids were now old enough to help and bring their friends.

We pulled into the driveway. The garage door was down, but I knew dad was home. The delicious aroma of something cooking reached our noses as soon as we got out of the car.

Dad answered the door quickly. He was always anxious for company since mom's death. A big smile spread across his face and settled in his eyes as he greeted us. My own smile widened as I realized how much I was loved. A happy feeling snuggled around me as I entered my childhood home.

"Hi, sweetie. Come in. How are you?" My dad leaned into a hug and kiss. "Hello, Harry. Good to see you. It's been too long." My father and Harry shook hands. Harry towered over my dad who was only about five feet, five inches tall. One look at my dad's full head of dark brown hair explained me. In old photos he looked like Dick Powell in 'The Thin Man' movies. His wiry body type gave me hope that I'd age like him. Of course, who'd want to be married to a wiry woman with hairy arms and a thin mustache? Well, Uncle Vinnie didn't mind, but his wife Edna could bake like an angel.

Dad brought us into the living room. Once we were settled he asked again, "I mean it Gracie, how are you. I saw the news last night."

"I'm fine, really. It was awful seeing that skeleton. Today it seems more pathetic than scary. That whole thing is really why we came over today." I stopped abruptly realizing how rude that sounded.

"And here I thought you came over to visit me or at least have a piece of homemade pizza, provided I take it out of the oven before it burns. Excuse me." Mike Morelli smiled broadly and hurried into the kitchen.

"Don't paint me with the same brush Mike," shouted Harry. I always come here for the food and the company."

My dad sauntered back into the room wearing one cow patterned oven mitt and holding the other. "I've got a few more minutes before it's ready. Now what were you saying ungrateful number one favorite daughter of aging father."

"Spare me the Charlie Chan. You know what I mean." He and I loved to tease each other. I was seven years old before I realized that being called his favorite daughter wasn't such high praise. I was his only daughter.

"Okay honey. What do you need?"

"I wondered if I could look through mom's things in the attic. I want to read Aunt Cecilia's diary again."

"What are you up to Gracie? Just a minute, my pizza's calling me."

I turned to Harry who was seated on the clear, plastic-covered love seat. "Why do people always think I'm up to something? If I didn't have such a healthy ego, I might take it personally." Harry gave me a slow exaggerated negative nod and deep shoulder shrug. He was exasperating at times. I was just about to tell him so when the chef *du jour* walked back into the room.

He placed a tray with coffee, hot water and tea bags and

Italian bakery on the coffee table and motioned us toward it. "Edna sent them over. Try the pizelles; they melt in your mouth. Take some home. I can't resist them and I gotta watch my girlish figure." He smiled and patted his barely rotund belly. "Everything is delicious. That woman can bake like an angel. So like I said," he continued without missing a beat, "what are you up to?"

"I'm not up to anything. I just wanted to read the diary and see what was happening around that time. You know maybe Aunt Cecilia talked about people and events and," my voice trailed off as I ran out of reasons.

"You never were a good liar, Gracie. Your eyes always gave you away." My dad was referring to my quirky physiology. When I was excited, nervous or scared, my lavender eyes turned pansy purple in an instant. I had been cursed with this barometer all my life.

"Dad," I interrupted.

He held up both hands in a gesture of surrender. "I know honey. You're not lying, you're searching for the right words." He smiled while Harry sputtered with laughter. I never could out do my father. "Gracie, all your mom's things are sorted in stacks up there. I've been working on going through all of it little by little. Let me take a look later on and I'll bring it to Mike's tonight. Right now, I have to bake my second pizza. The seniors' club is having a pizza party tomorrow and I'm down for the pizzas."

"What's everybody else bringing?" Harry asked.

"The party I guess," Dad answered. We laughed at his deadpan humor.

"Thanks Dad, love you. See you later." A big hug and kiss accompanied all the words. Harry and Dad shook hands and we were out the door.

CHAPTER SEVEN

Karen's two messages were on our machine. She wanted to meet for a drink. I called back and we agreed to meet at The Braxton. It's about halfway for both of us. Karen lived in Oak Park and it would take her a little longer since she usually took the wrong exit at Route 83 and ended up having to make a U-turn and retrace her route. She looked so competent; people always stop to ask *her* for directions. She usually told them she was new in town to avoid getting them lost. In her case, not only could you not take Oak Park out of the girl, but you couldn't take the girl out of Oak Park.

Karen had attended Trinity High School, Regina College and then taken a job teaching at Trinity. She had no interest in pursuing the study abroad opportunity our junior year. Most of us couldn't wait to go, but she never traveled far afield. During the football season, Regina and Notre Dame would arrange for the Regina 'beads' (the local nickname) to ride the bus to Notre Dame's campus, go to the stadium for the game, and then stay for the dance. I guess the weekends were engineered to mix and match available Catholic men and women. The girls attending St. Mary's, across the lake from Notre Dame, were not thrilled when that motor coach carrying all us interlopers pulled in each Saturday. They had another nickname for us that also started with a 'b'. Karen never joined the weekly pilgrimages to Notre Dame. My theory was that she felt guilty about being out of town the weekend her mother died in a boating accident. She had opted to go hiking with a friend at Starved Rock State Park instead of sailing with her mother. Elizabeth Kramer had taken her 32-foot sailboat out alone. Karen had never stopped with the 'what ifs.

The Braxton wasn't crowded which allowed us to sit easily in the comfortable high-backed chairs in the lounge and talk about the Rosary Bride until we ordered our second vodka tonics. "Sister Andrew thinks she recorded something about odd happenings around that time. But she admits that Pearl Harbor disrupted her writing routine."

"Grace, you remember my aunt, don't you? She was at Regina around that time. I remember hearing stories about how they all rolled bandages and filled first aid kits to be sent overseas. I also remember her complaining about the shortage of silk stockings. Most of their boyfriends were in the Service. I guess they had lots of time to roll bandages and complain. Ric and I are invited for dinner tonight. I'll see if she remembers anything unusual. I'd love to scoop Ric on uncovering the bride's identity."

"Well, that won't take much. Apparently, they are in no rush to assign manpower to such an old case. I'd just like to know the truth. I keep getting these feelings. I can't explain them, that maybe the skeleton is the remains of my aunt. She disappeared from Regina around that time."

"I don't know Grace. That would be too bizarre."

"Tell me about it," I sighed. "I just can't shake this feeling. In the alcove the other day, I screamed when you came in because I could feel something in that room with me. I think it was her."

"Gracie, take it easy, honey. You were in shock." Karen

reached across the table to squeeze my hand. I had completed my third row of braiding in the time we had been talking.

"I know. Harry said the same thing. She did go to Regina though for two years before she disappeared. My mother wanted so much to find her and all the College could ever tell her was that she simply up and left one day, with no word to anyone. They mailed a letter they found in her room to mother's Aunt Fiona, but it didn't say much more. Her diary had all kinds of information about her life at school and it just didn't jive with college's version. December 6, 1941 was her last entry. She wrote about her Presentation Tea."

"Her what?" interrupted Karen.

"Presentation Tea. You know. Remember Sister A telling us about the tradition they had about weddings. The girls would schedule an afternoon tea with the nuns so they could see the bride's finery. Since the nuns could rarely attend the weddings it was a lovely way for them to feel included."

"Oh, like a bachelorette party with God," Karen quipped.

"You are a nostalgia monger aren't you," I countered. "And God will get you for that."

"Just kidding. It does sound nice. So, you think because the diary mentions her tea that your aunt wasn't in the frame of mind to run away. It makes sense. What if something happened in the next few days that really changed her mind or her feelings? Maybe she just didn't write it down."

"I know, I've thought of that. With my mother gone, I can't even confirm these feelings or ideas. Maybe I should just let the whole thing go. Harry and I stopped by my dad's earlier and I asked him to find Cecilia's diary and bring it to Mike's house tonight. I just wish I could talk to my mom."

Karen must have guessed my thought. She put her hand over mine. "I know Gracie. It's hard to lose your mom. You think you're going to have all the time in the world together and then you don't."

I squeezed her hand. "Thanks. Gotta' run. I'll see you tomorrow."

"Bring the diary, okay? I thought maybe you had it in that bag." She pointed to the bag on the floor between our chairs.

"Oh, brother. I can't believe I was going to leave and forget to return this to you." I lifted the bag onto my lap and pulled out the creamy, white sweater. "Thanks. It was warm. I love the design. It's old isn't it?"

"It is. My aunt gave it to me. She wore it when she was at Regina. Someone brought it back from Ireland for her, I think. I guess that pattern was all the rage back then."

"I know. My mom had one just like it and she got it from her aunt in Ireland. I wonder if it's with her things. I'd love to have it. I'll have to call my dad. Well, thanks again."

"Sure thing." She smiled and left the table carrying the sweater over her arm. I folded the Lord & Taylor bag and tucked it under my arm. It was my turn to pick up the tab. I walked out five minutes after Karen, just in time to see her turn the wrong way out of the parking lot.

When I got home, Harry told me that Betty Dulaney from the college had called. She had checked her fiche and all she had on Don Martin was an address in Oak Park. The record indicated that he had moved to Florida. Harry had written down the address and thanked her for her efforts.

A glance at my watch told me that we were expected at my brother's house for dinner in less than two hours. My oldest nephew was leaving for his study abroad and this was his going away get-together.

Harry had fit right in with my family when he first met

them. He came from a small family. His twin sister, Hannah still lived in England with his parents. My in-laws were very sweet, gentle, people. They used to visit more often, but the years and the horrible time when Harry was gone took a toll on their health. William Marsden had suffered a heart attack five years ago. At seventy-six, he had recovered nicely, but still tired easily and liked to stay close to home. Harry's mother, Dorothy, never liked traveling very much so we were planning a long visit at Christmas. In lieu of nearby family, Harry immersed himself in my rather noisy and sometimes pushy crowd. After all, we were Irish and Italian. Harry said that made us loud and stubborn.

I was the middle child with two older brothers and two younger brothers. At any point in my life, I was either a nagging little sister or an adored big sister. I am a Gemini, which probably accounts for the *versatility or duality of my personality* or so says the fortune cookie I choose to quote.

Tonight I would be cast in the role of Auntie Gem. The brother who so dubbed me married young and had two sons in quick order, their boys, Jeff, and Joseph, have always called me Auntie Gem. Dinner tonight was for Jeffrey who was a sophomore at Champaign. I had pitched Regina, but he wanted no part of a small Liberal Arts college. Maybe I'd have better luck with Joseph, the next college-bound Morelli.

"Harry, do you want me to shower first? We have to get going or we'll be late. Actually, we're bringing the appetizers, so we ought to be a little early. Carolyn said dinner at 7:00."

"Let's shower together and save time," Harry proposed as he stepped out of his trousers. Who was he kidding?

CHAPTER EIGHT

The Chinese popovers were almost thawed. I carefully packed several platters so I could arrange them for nuking at Mike's house. Most of the Morellis would be there, so I made a triple batch. My oldest brother, Joseph, a priest in Seattle, wouldn't be there, but my two younger brothers and their families would be joining us. Marty was married to Eve and they had one daughter, my godchild, Katherine Grace. Glen was divorced, but had custody of his three boys.

Harry carried the platters and was already out of the house when the telephone rang. I was holding two bowls of Chinese popovers and trying to flip the switch with my elbow. The door was swinging closed behind me and I knew I couldn't catch it in time. Maybe they'd leave a message.

Dinner was great fun. We laughed and told goofy stories. The kids always enjoyed hearing the silly tales of their folks when they were younger and I liked hearing them too. My niece and nephews grew up with "Mick the Monster" stories. Sometimes, during our family stories, the older kids drew parallels between life and art. I told each child that their dad inspired "Mick the Monster." Of course, Jeff and Joey always thought it was their dad because the family had called Mike 'Mickey' since he was a baby. Much to his credit, he tolerated that nickname until he hit high school but during his teens, he begged us to call him Mike. It took years for all the relatives to remember to use 'Mike'. My entire family seemed to use aliases. I called one cousin Chickie for years until I was invited to the wedding of someone named Kathleen. My cousin Jimmy was really Vincent. My Uncle Shorty was really Elmer. Well, that I could understand. It wasn't just my father's family. My mother's Christian name of Margaret had mutated to Peg. Even Great Aunt Fiona's brother Jacob had become Jack in this country. They had some nerve to criticize our lifestyle. At least we knew our names.

This particular night however everyone seemed to want to talk about the skeleton behind the fireplace.

"Auntie Gem, Dad says you know the Inspector on the case. Did he tell you anything?" Jeff waited for an answer. All the adults looked everywhere except at me.

"Sorry, Sis," Mike said quietly. "What's everybody looking at?" I just wanted to know if Auntie Gem got any inside information."

"Nothing wrong with that! Out with it, Darling. What have you learned from the constabulary?" Harry's carefree tone cut the tension. I flashed him a grateful smile and retold my meeting with Ric, leaving out some of graphic details and all of the personal ones. My narrative lead to some wild theories.

"Grace, I remember a story about a ghost students used to see roaming the halls. Wasn't that in Power?" Carolyn, my sister-in-law, had graduated from Regina two years before me. Yes, it was," I answered slowly. I was remembering my feelings in the alcove.

"The students nicknamed her the Rosary Bride," continued Carolyn. "I guess that's how the media picked up the name."

The ghost talk continued, as Carolyn recounted another

story. "The story that scared me half to death when I lived there was the one about the nun who stepped into the elevator shaft and fell to her death. The elevator manufacturer said it would have been impossible to open the iron grate door if the elevator car wasn't at that floor. After that mysterious death students living closest to the elevator swore they heard the whine of the motor as the elevator inched its way to the third floor. They'd hear the clank of the gears when the car stopped, the squeaking of the iron door as it was pulled open and then the awful scream. The school officials wrote that off to hysteria brought on by the sound of the elevator. Eventually, the dormitory rooms were reassigned and the rooms closest to the elevator were used as storage space or study halls. That elevator was overhauled and the old gear and pulley variety replaced with a quiet hydraulic car with sliding paneled doors. During the 1970's, when I was there, enrollment skyrocketed and the school remodeled the old rooms for use as dormitories. Three weeks after the first students took those rooms, the residents living closest to the elevator heard the exact same sounds as their predecessors had all those years before. They swore they heard clanking and squeaking sounds followed by a horrible scream."

Carolyn paused for dramatic effect. My niece's eyes were the size of saucers and her cousin Joey had moved closer to her in an effort to put someone in between himself and the storyteller.

The silence was broken by Eve, my other sister-in-law, when she started a ghost story from her college dorm days. "Every school seems to have a skeleton or two," stated Eve. "At Wesleyan everyone whispered about the haunting of the Delta's house. It seemed that back in the forties, when the sorority had to tear down the old carriage house, workers found remains of a skeleton. Apparently, the carriage house had been a very popular spot for young Deltas in love." Eve paused to sip her tonic.

"A college library is hardly a spot for a tryst," interrupted Carolyn. "The Regina skeleton couldn't have been there by choice."

"That's true," agreed Eve. "But maybe she led some guy to the brink and back again and he reacted badly. Anyway, getting back to the Deltas, the girls in the house swore that they would get feelings in certain parts of the house, drops in temperature, unusual smells, stuff like that. The college was upset with all the stories popping up about the identity of the skeleton. I guess every missing person that had ever been reported in that area *became* that skeleton at one point or another."

I cringed as I listened to Eve. *Was I overreacting by looking for my aunt in Regina's skeleton? Harry and I had agreed not to mention my theory. The entire family suffered enough as we stood by helplessly watching our gentle mother anguish over the loss of her sister. Mom never got over not knowing about her sister, her only sibling. I think that's one reason she had so many children. Well, that and the fact that she was Catholic.* My thoughts were interrupted as Eve continued her story.

"Finally, the college was able to track the property back to early settler days and guess what they found out?" Eve waited a dramatic moment and then added, "The College had built the carriage house on the site of an old cemetery!"

"Eghhh," wailed Kate. "Mother, that's gross." After a few more spectral stories, someone brought up Chicago's famous Resurrection Mary. Harry usually encouraged ghost talk and always added a few druid stories of his own, but tonight he was uncharacteristically quiet and the party soon broke up.

Just before the tall tales shrank down to size, my dad motioned me toward the kitchen.

"Here's the diary you wanted, Honey. Your mother and I read it over and over, from cover to cover through the years trying to make some sense of Cecilia's disappearance. There's nothing in the whole thing that points to any answer. But it's yours if you want it."

"Thanks, Dad. I just want to look it over myself. You're a dear. Thanks." I leaned into his open arms and returned his hug.

"There you are." My brother Mike put an arm around me and squeezed. "Thanks for the popovers, they're my favorite." Hugs and kisses later, and after the last good-byes Harry and I joined Marty and Eve for drinks at the Palm Court. Their daughter, Kate was spending the night with Mike's family.

Our table faced Arlington Heights Road. Harry and Eve ordered bitters (Harry loved the stuff; Eve was an anglophile). Marty *saluded* my vodka and tonic with his Michelob. "What's up Gracie? You barely talked at Mike's."

At Marty's coaxing, I told him and Eve my suspicions. "Grace, that would be too—" Eve stopped, at a loss for words.

"Bizarre?" I finished. "That's what Karen said. Why couldn't it be her? The time is right."

"Grace, I feel terrible about what I said earlier. I'm sorry, I had no idea how you felt."

"Eve, don't be silly. How could you possibly know? Don't worry, I'm not upset."

"C'mon, we're all tired. Let's finish our drinks and go home. Things will make more sense tomorrow." Good advice from a younger brother. When we finally made it home, Harry and I both ignored the blinking red eye on the answering machine, too tired to care who had called. That was the first mistake.

I woke up suddenly and for no apparent reason. I hate when that happens. Harry wasn't in bed. I listened for sounds from the bathroom or kitchen. Nothing. I walked through the den to the kitchen. I noticed that the message light was out. I tried to retrieve the message but it had been erased. Now I was curious. It was 4:30 in the morning. What on earth was going on? I saw the note propped against the Bunn.

Darling, hope to be back before you're out of bed. Love, Harry. Harry knew the first thing I did once my eyes were open (sometimes even before) was brew coffee. So, that's what I did. Obviously, I wasn't going back to sleep. I wanted to get an early start on the diary. I hadn't thought it would be this early. I picked up the diary from the counter and carried my cup of coffee into the library. My favorite reading chair was an overstuffed affair with wide flat arms for papers, books, and the mandatory cup of coffee. I settled in, tucked my legs under me, and diligently started reading from page one.

My aunt's handwriting was small, precise, and very easy to read. I realized she must have started the diary when she first arrived at Regina in the fall of 1939 when she worked in the dining room to earn money for her expenses. Eventually, she was asked to serve in the Sisters' dining room, which was an honor of a kind. Her own words said, *"I am so thrilled. Can you imagine that? I told them I'd be ever so honored to serve the Sisters."* Some of her descriptions and stories about the nuns were hilarious. The next few pages covered more school events and comments on different classmates. Her entries were brief and almost automatic, as though a task she performed as habit. I flipped a few pages at a time until I found a longer entry. Cecilia was offered the position of Tea Mistress. There was quite a bit on that.

Then I spotted something I could relate to. Cecilia was writing about the tunnels. Her account must be of tunnels long since closed off because I didn't recognize the location. I did recall that there was an entrance to the underground tunnels from the Chapel Garden. Once inside the garden, the door on the left led to a subbasement with tunnels that crisscrossed the entire college. Access to the dormitory was easy at that point. Cecilia had one of the old servant's rooms that had been converted into a dorm room when the kitchen behind Power Hall was remodeled. One tunnel beneath the kitchen provided access to a dumbwaiter that happened to stop in what used to be the 'tidy-up' room for the serving girls. This dormant dumbwaiter opened into a tiny room with a sink, buckets, and mops. Girls made sure that the latch was off so they could sneak their boyfriends into their rooms.

According to the diary, Cecilia discovered the 'underground' one day while emptying teapots. She described a time when she nearly died of fright. While washing out some tea things, she heard the squeak of the old pulley. She turned and saw a man backing into the room. Of course, the young man was almost as frightened as Cecilia when he turned expecting to see his girlfriend and saw a wide-eyed woman with a teapot held over her head like a club. Just at that moment the girlfriend rushed in, explained the system to Cecilia, swore her to secrecy, and took her boyfriend away to her room.

I was really enjoying reading my aunt's words, seeing a different side of her. My mother's recollections of her sister were from their childhood in Ireland. My grandparents had been killed in an automobile accident when my mother was seven and Cecilia was twelve. Their great aunt took charge of their upbringing. Aunt Fiona was extremely religious and had little tolerance for young girls and their silly ways. When my mother described those early years, they often sounded tense and unhappy. Cecilia had been her best friend and shining star. I flipped through pages, skimming lines here and there. A summer entry caught my attention.

> *Dear Diary, The dormitories will be closed for two weeks this summer. I'm lucky to be able to stay with Sheila. Her dad is an important lawyer in the city of Chicago. He rides the train every morning to a fancy building where he has his office. I love their house. It's so grand and beautiful. I'll have my own room as one of her sisters is in New York City for the summer. Sheila's the last of three girls to attend Regina. I wonder if my little Maggie will follow in her big Sis's footsteps and come to Regina. Anyway, everything is set. Sister Phillip told Mrs. Conners that it would be ever so fine for 'Sheila' to stay with them. What a lark! Even Sister can't keep our names straight. I guess we Irish all look alike to her.*

I laughed aloud at her sense of humor. Now her diary was filled with descriptions of the house, her room, the family, and one family friend in particular. It was in the Conners' home that Cecilia first met Thomason. According to her text, Tommy, as he was known to his friends, had graduated from law school, and was home for a summer of rest and relaxation before he began clerking for Mr. Conners. Cecilia and Tommy seemed to have become mutually engrossed in each other. She confided to her diary.

> *I cannot stop looking at him. He's the most handsome lad I've ever seen. When he smiles at me, I cannot hardly breathe.*

I found myself raising my hand to my throat to express her words. I knew from my mother that she and her sister sounded almost identical. My mother's voice had a light, sparkling tone that filled her conversation with the sound of tinkling wind chimes set in motion by a new story to tell. I sat back now and heard the words come to life.

The next few pages described her continued romance with Tommy. One date was at Peterson's Ice Cream Shoppe. Another entry described swimming at Oak Street Beach. Her entries were longer. She devoted more time to details. Perhaps her studies or tea duties were being crowded by her desire to record every exciting moment of her new relationship.

I spotted a new name, Karl Bauer, and read more closely.

> *Dear Diary, Karl asked me the strangest question today. He wanted to know why my boyfriend never walks me to the gate and waits with me until Karl can open it. After curfew the big gates are locked and you have to ring the bell for someone to open it. I've missed curfew only a few times. I know some girls who miss it every time. Tommy would like that. He's always fussin' at me that I care what the nuns say and think. Tommy says that girls who really care about their fellows don't listen to the nuns. Well, I was so surprised when Karl asked me that. He said the other fellows would never leave their girlfriends standing on the pavement waiting in the dark. What if he didn't hear the bell? What if he weren't there at all? His questions bother me a little.*

I never thought about it, but Tommy never does walk me up. Sometimes he lets me off from his car two blocks away so the nuns think I've taken the streetcar. Karl is one of the few people on campus that's even seen Tommy. I think I'll ask Tommy to walk me up from now on.

I didn't know who this Karl was but he apparently stirred up my aunt. It sounded like her knight in shinning armor had a rust spot. A tiny one, but none the less, a spot. No woman wanted to think that her man didn't want to protect her or that he was embarrassed to be seen with her.

Speaking of *man*, where was mine. I was pouring my fourth cup when the telephone rang. The noise startled me and I jerked my hand. Piping hot coffee splashed over the rim of the cup and burned my hand.

"Dammit!" My quick dash to the sink to run my hand under cold water probably saved my life. I heard a light tinkle and a solid thud almost simultaneously. I knew the sound. A bullet had buried itself somewhere in a wall very near me. I ran back into the library and darkness, grabbing for the telephone as the recorder kicked in.

"Wait! Help! Please don't hang up," I'm shouting. My desperate words were hurried and garbled compared to the outgoing message playing to the caller.

"Grace!"

"Harry! Oh, God! Harry, help me. Someone's outside."

"Hang up and hide. I'm ten minutes away. I'll call the police."

"Hurry!"

"Go!" He ordered.

I ran across the library to the fireplace wall. Three yards

away from the fireplace I heard glass breaking. My fingers finally reached one of the stones in the fireplace. I twisted it left and heard the slight click. The panel directly in front of me slid open noiselessly. I hurried inside and turned to push the lever to close the panel. A split second before it closed a cautious beam of light moved across the room.

I tried to control my breathing, fearing that my gasping would be heard through the wall. Little by little my breathing slowed. I couldn't hear anything from the other side of the panel. The secret room was only a small cubby measuring 4' x 6' and barely five and a half feet high. I knew that for fact since my 5'4" frame just made it without slamming my forehead against the stone facade. Minutes ticked by stretching my nerves as the silence wrapped around me and began to tighten its grip. The original purpose of the room was to hide the priest ministering to Church of England nobles who in reality practiced Catholicism. Many a priest retained his life and many a nobleman retained his title because of the quick disappearing trick. The room was light proof. It seemed like forever waiting in the darkness. I started to feel lightheaded. I knew these types of rooms weren't supposed to be airtight. After all, the priest had to be able to breathe until he could come out. Did our builder know that? The air was close and there was a smell. An old smell, musty like decay. We didn't store anything in here. The air was warm now. The smell grew stronger. I felt clammy and faint. Suddenly a shock of cold air chilled my sweaty body. The chill rose out of the stone floor, seeped into my slippers, and crawled up my legs. I held my hand over my mouth afraid a gasp would give me away. In the silence, I heard a soft breath. The cold increased. I shivered in my lightweight sleep shirt. I strained my eyes trying to pierce the darkness of the wall a mere six feet from me. Another sound reached my ears. I heard a siren, first faintly, then stronger, until finally I heard pounding on the door.

"Hello! Hello! Mrs. Marsden. Police! Let us in. Can you let us in?" I didn't know if I should leave my hiding place. I felt a presence with me. I knew the police were outside, but what if someone was still inside the house, maybe even standing on the other side of this panel? My panic mounted when I realized that the pounding had stopped.

"Oh, God, they wouldn't leave!" Fear made my decision. I pushed the lever and the panel slid open. Two steps into the room, I realized there was someone there. The flashlight beam moved around to my end of the room. I turned to run. My hip bumped into the desk. He whirled and saw me. The beam jumped to the level of my eyes. In the moment before I was blinded by the glare, I saw the gun.

Chapter Nine

The first glow of sunrise boldly lit up the kitchen by the time the police left. When I hadn't answered their knocks, they tried the back door. They found the broken windowpane in the French door from the patio. The two officers had separated. One went around to the front door again. Patrolman Peterson had entered cautiously and proceeded through the den into the library. He thought he had the intruder when he whirled around after hearing me bump into the desk. I felt as though I'd been part of a police academy training clip where the cardboard figures pop up and the trainee has a split second to shoot or hold.

After explanations and apologies, they called a forensic team to the house. The doors and windows on the back of the house were dusted for fingerprints. Two officers carefully searched the area around the house, but the dry, hard ground yielded no footprints. I noticed a third officer ranging the yard on his own. He seemed familiar, maybe he had patrolled the compound before, or maybe his moonlighting job was some kind of tradesman. We had plenty of those through here. He hung back as the other two came into the kitchen. They surmised that the perpetrator made it out the side door through the garage during the time that the officers were at the front door. The small door in the garage faces the back of the property and was wide open when the police checked the house. Easy for someone to slip away toward the band of woods and the golf course beyond that.

A small caliber bullet removed from the wall had left a larger ragged hole that I couldn't help envisioning in me. My hands sought out the purple braid I had used as a bookmark.

Sergeant Roy, who arrived with forensics, took my statement. I tried my best to answer his questions precisely and fully, but everything had happened so quickly and I was still shaken. I could barely remember the proper sequence. The last question he asked won the toss as the most difficult to answer.

"Mrs. Marsden, do you know any reason why someone would want to harm you?"

It wasn't difficult because there was a long list open for speculation, but because I'd never thought in terms of someone wanting to hurt me. I was on the eighth loop of my braid. I had to complete ten before I could answer. I couldn't formulate an answer until I completed ten. Nine. The silence continued. Sergeant Roy looked at me. Ten.

"No, of course I don't," I stammered. He proceeded to ask questions about my friends, my work, and my family. Nothing made sense.

"I write children's books for heaven's sake. Who'd be upset with me? Even a bad review wouldn't warrant this." I raised both my hands, palm up, to encompass the kitchen and event in an effort at humor. Nothing made sense.

Sergeant Roy acknowledged my nervousness with a slight smile. He explained that he'd file the report as a random home invasion. He felt that perhaps my appearance in the kitchen had startled the burglar, who panicked and fired at me to insure his escape.

Harry seemed anxious to hurry the Sergeant out the door.

Finally Sergeant Roy snapped shut his notebook and assured me that they would assign extra patrols and call me as soon as they developed any leads. Harry shook his hand and closed the door behind him.

"Bloody idiot," he exploded.

"I know. He didn't seem to believe anything I told him. If they hadn't found that bullet, he might have chalked this up to a bad dream or too much caf—"

"Not him. Me. I'm the bloody idiot."

"What are you talking about?" Suddenly the security of daylight and the normalcy of coffee in my kitchen flooded through my being. I remembered the reason I had been awake earlier. "And where did you go. Something woke me. You weren't there. Your note said nothing." I looked around and saw it on the counter.

"You fell asleep so quickly last night and I was a little restless. I remembered I hadn't checked the machine for the call that came in when we were leaving. That one was a hang-up. The next call got me dressed and fifty miles away from you like a stupid fool! The caller said he was Derek." Harry stopped when he heard my intake of breath.

"Well, obviously it wasn't Derek," he continued. "But it was someone who knew I'd leave, no questions asked, and drive an hour to meet him."

"Harry, it's been almost five years since you've even heard from Derek."

"I know, I know. I wanted to believe the voice was Derek's. It sounded like him. Somebody wanted me out of the house in order to make it easier to get to you. What in God's name is going on, Gracie? Who wants to hurt you?"

"Maybe someone was trying to scare me or something," my voice trailed off as I tried not to think about someone wanting me dead. "This is crazy." I stood up and walked to the French doors. The broken glass had been swept up. "Nobody wants me dead! Maybe Sergeant Roy is right. Maybe I did surprise a burglar."

I don't know if either of us believed that, but we both pretended to at the moment.

"I'm going up to shower. I'm meeting Karen for breakfast to find out what she learned from her aunt."

"I'll be up in a jiffy. I want to call London. Someone should be able to check up on Derek for me. Don't worry, Darling. We'll get to the bottom of this."

Harry's comment stuck with me as I climbed the stairs to our bedroom. The past few hours had seemed like a nightmare sequence, like falling from a rooftop and I didn't want to hit bottom.

CHAPTER TEN

Two hours later, with not enough sleep and even less make-up, I met Karen for breakfast. She took one look at my bare, strained features, and expressed her concern with, "You look awful Grace. Is everything okay between you and Harry?" Just like Karen to assume, any trouble would be marital. She had a low opinion of marriage since hers crashed and burned.

Right after graduation Karen had thrown herself into her new career. She worked incessantly teaching full time and tutoring summers. Her aunt finally convinced her to take the summer off and travel with her to Europe to celebrate Karen's 25th birthday and Aunt Shelley's 50th. When I turned twenty-five my family gave me a gift certificate to the Magic Pan restaurant and a Spa Day at Mario Tricocci. That was as European as it got for me.

She met a young businessman on board the cruise ship and they continued their relationship when they arrived in Europe. He was from Chicago and had actually met her Uncle Richard at a law convention. Small world. They dated for a short time and were married within months. Most of Karen's friends were surprised at her rush to the altar. She had never really dated much in spite of her aunt's best efforts to line up eligible men. I remember that one of her would be suitors had the bad taste and worse fortune to suggest the reason he didn't 'score' with

Karen was because she leaned toward an alternative lifestyle. The young man had hoped for a career with a prestigious Chicago brokerage firm. Uncle Richard called a friend. The young man left town.

This young man seemed perfect: successful, Irish and from good stock. Aunt Shelly hadn't handpicked him, but he apparently checked out. Within weeks, the wedding was planned. I was her maid of honor and only attendant. Her aunt shepherded us around like a savvy sheep dog 'breaking in' two frisky lambs. We bought our dresses at Gilmore's in Oak Park. Aunt Shelly had final say so on everything.

Karen's wedding reception had been at the Oak Park Arms and boasted a guest list that included the finest families. No one from my family was invited. Her aunt had said she just couldn't squeeze another person in.

Karen was married with all the hoopla accorded a minor princess. Seven months later she moved back home after an unpleasant and expensive separation. I suspect Uncle Richard exerted some legal muscle through his old law firm and finished the divorce quickly. He also managed to keep her inheritance intact. Prenuptial agreements weren't in vogue then. Aunt Shelly delivered an annulment from the Archdiocese in record time. Within the year, it was almost as if *he* had never happened.

We never talked about it much, but I supposed that she realized she couldn't force herself into an uncomfortable lifestyle just to please her aunt and society. Especially her aunt. Karen was devoted to her and really sought her approval. They discussed everything. It was no surprise to me that she expected marital mayhem as the cause of my lousy appearance.

I explained the events of a few hours ago. Karen was stunned. She asked the same questions that Harry and I had asked each other.

"Harry said he would try to reach someone in London about Derek. Maybe he's the connection to this mess. He and Derek made many enemies. Maybe this is some kind of payback. I don't know everything that happened in that prison. Harry doesn't talk about it. When he had been release from the hospital and realized that Derek had been left behind, he wouldn't rest until Derek was released. He was ready to go back there himself, but, thank God, the paper channels worked that time."

"Yeah, but Derek believed that Harry knew he was left behind," Karen interrupted. "Didn't he blame Harry for cutting a deal for his own release and leaving him to rot?"

"Actually, he blamed me and your uncle for negotiating Harry's release at his expense. When he was released he wouldn't return Harry's calls, wouldn't talk to him when Harry tried to visit him in the hospital. Derek's wife and son left him shortly after he returned. He blamed us for that too. I don't know, maybe it's connected."

I put both my hands on the back of my neck and rubbed the spot at the base and then across the top of my shoulders. "Let's talk about your aunt," I said, changing the subject.

"Well, shouldn't you have a bodyguard or something?"

"The police think I interrupted a burglar and that I'm safe now."

"But still."

"Very discreetly glance near the door."

My friend turned slightly, pretending to look out the window.

"So Harry does have a guardian angel for you." Karen was referring to a middle-aged man seated near the door. She recognized him as Walter, Harry's masseur. Walter was built like a dwarf oak tree. He was barrel-chested with forearms and hands that were big and burley. When he stood up his legs looked like they had rooted to the spot and only a gale force wind could uproot him.

Because of injuries Harry had suffered in prison, he needed the therapeutic benefits of a daily massage. Walter stopped in at the house every day. In addition to the massage, he sometimes ran errands for Harry or did odd jobs around the house. He was very strong and very devoted to Harry. There were reasons other than the usual employer/employee relationship, but neither talked about them. When he arrived this morning, Harry asked him to skip the massage and tag along with me for the day. I fought the idea until I saw how serious Harry was. Admittedly, there was a certain comfort in knowing that someone was within close reach.

"So you see, nothing to worry about." I dismissed her concern with a shrug. "Now, come on. What did your aunt remember?"

"Actually, not much. I told her about Sister Andrew's ideas. My aunt said she remembered very little of that time; so long ago and all. We both saw Sister A yesterday. She was walking back from the Priory and we gave her a ride to Regina. I couldn't believe how spry she looked. I'd hate to power walk with her. What a coincidence. I know you've kept in touch with her, but I haven't seen her in years. Aunt Shelly and Sister had quite a chat since I had to stop at school and drop off new English Literature tests. Sister probably could have made it to Regina faster on foot."

"What about your Uncle Richard? He was around then."

"Truthfully Grace, I didn't talk to him much. He was busy directing the Bears defense with Ric most of the time. I still can't get excited about football. So I guess we're at a standstill."

"Maybe not. I'm going back to Regina to talk with Sister Andrew. Maybe she'll remember more today. I brought my aunt's diary to show Sister. If this doesn't jog her memory and shake loose anything more, I'm stopping at the newspaper office to search their morgue. This might be the end of the search for our *bride*."

"Have you read any of this yet? Anything good?" Karen grinned as she reached for the book on the table next to my coffee cup.

"It depends what you mean by good. I think I was just getting to a good part when all hell broke loose last night, ah this morning. I haven't had the chance to pick it up again." I directed Karen to the last pages I had read. I pulled out the purple braid I had used as a bookmark. She started reading aloud.

Dear Diary, tomorrow will be a very important day for me. I will be going to meet Tommy's father and brother! We're driving up to their cottage to spend the weekend. Tommy says he's never brought a girl up to the cottage, 'cause that's just for family. I only wish I could have him meet Aunt Fiona and my precious Maggie. Wish me luck. I hope they approve.

"I can't believe she's nervous about their approval. What about them meeting her approval?" Karen asked. "This subservient attitude is exactly why it took so long for changes to come about for women," she preached.

"Get off your soap box and keep reading."

Karen turned the page and continued the narrative. "Dear Diary, this weekend is the best weekend of my life. It didn't start out that way. It started out as a sham. His father and brother weren't at the cottage. No one was! He tricked me. At first, I'm furious with him for lying to me and I tell him to take me back to school. I know he is up to no good and I did not budge from the car. Then my whole life changes and I am stepping out of the car and onto cloud nine. He tells me he would never bring me up here if his intentions were not honorable. He is truly hurt that I thought the worst of him. I guess all that talk from Karl, the school custodian, had confused me."

"Who's Karl?" Karen stopped reading to ask.

"I'll tell you later. Keep going."

"Tommy shows me the big living room and talks about *our* children playing on that very floor. We sat down on the couch and he tells me all about his dad and brother. He says he wishes his mother were alive to meet me. I am just the sort of girl she would have wanted for a daughter-in-law. About this time, he is all choked up about his mother. Not many men are so sensitive. I know that a man likes to be strong in front of his girlfriend, so I change the subject and ask him for a drink of water. He brings back a whiskey and water sort of drink. It tastes awful but Tommy says it's what all his crowd at law school drinks. He calls it an *acquired taste.* Then he shows me the last room in the cottage. His bedroom! We promise undying love to each other. I want to wait, but Tommy says it would be better to make love now so we can get used to each other. I want to make him happy, but I still know we should wait. I tell him, absolutely not. He agrees to just cuddle and kiss. His caresses are gentle and warm and then he opens my blouse, I blush in his arms. His lips feel rough on my soft skin and I think I would die of pleasure. I feel all giddy and lightheaded as Tommy holds my weight while I lean back into his arms. He says I'm beautiful and he has to love me or he'll burst."

"I'm going to burst!" exploded Karen. I don't believe this. I know she was your aunt, but for heaven's sake she was as naive as a turnip."

"Karen, we're talking fifty years ago. Everybody was naive. "Now keep going. My mother never told me any of this."

"Of course she wouldn't. If you read between the lines, your aunt is describing her own rape. The worst part is she never knew it was rape. I'll bet money there was more in that whiskey than just water.

"Hand it over. Maybe I can get through it." I motioned for the diary. "Besides, I certainly can't let Sister Andrew read this part. I'll have to clip these pages together." I adjusted the book on my side of the table and continued.

"I tell him no. He tells me he loves me, because I am a good girl. Tommy refreshes our drinks and kisses me on my neck lifting my hair to nibble at my earlobe. I want to button my blouse but he asks me to leave it undone because I look so sexy. I am so excited by what he said but I know he wants me to leave my blouse undone for another reason. He wants to touch me inside my clothes. This way he won't lose control is how he explains it. When he puts his hand on my knee and moves it under my skirt I want to jump out of my skin. There seems no harm in this. I hear some of the girls talk about touching through their clothes. My arms and legs are like lead though and Tommy helps me to lie down. My head is so heavy and my eyes won't stay open. I can still hear him telling me he loves me and we'll be married soon. He says he's going to undress me and tuck me under the covers for a nap. I didn't remember anything else until the next morning."

"I told you," Karen whispered triumphantly. "This Tommy was a real scum bag."

"Will you be quiet," I admonished. "There's only a little more writing under this entry. Want me to finish or not?"

"Okay go ahead," Karen mumbled. I cleared my throat and fixed Karen with a *you'd better be quiet look.*

"That next morning I thought my life was over. I wake up alone and I know in an instant that I gave myself to Tommy. I sinned and caused him to sin with me. I fear that he is disgusted with me and left me there alone in my shame. Suddenly, I hear whistling from the other room. It's Tommy! He hasn't left me at all. I can see him from the doorway. The kitchen table is set and he is scooping coffee into the percolator. The door creaks as I move it and Tommy turns toward the sound. 'Good morning', he says as he walks up to me and kisses me nice and gentle. He smiles and tells me breakfast will be ready in a few minutes. Oh joy! I am thinking I am a ruined woman and here he is treating me like Sunday best. I am truly the luckiest girl in the world."

"You're right Karen. This guy was slick. My aunt's letters home were filled with news of Tommy. Now I see how those letters were edited. My mother must have been devastated when she first read this. In one letter she wrote to my mom, Cecilia described the weekend at the cottage, but included the father and brother and the marriage proposal. Subsequent letters mentioned her 'secret' wedding plans."

"Secret?" Karen interrupted.

"Oh yes. Listen to this. He made her promise not to tell anyone about their wedding plans because he had enlisted in the Army and he didn't want people to think he was a *cad* by marrying her and dashing off to serve God and country. He was slick all right. You know what though, Karen? My mother told me once that when she read that letter she thought the idea of a secret engagement was romantic. I guess it was their generation. I personally think after reading this he needed to keep her willing to *play house* with him. I'm certain the cottage wasn't their one and only time."

"I'm sure," agreed Karen. "He probably used those tunnels just like the other guys. How are you not going to show those pages to Sister Andrew? I mean if she wants you to leave the diary what are you going to do, glue the pages shut?" Karen smiled as she posed the question.

"You're right. I can't show this to her. I'll just ask her if she remembered anything. Maybe I'll just mention some general stuff."

"Call me and let me know."

"Sure thing. Oh, Karen?"

"What?"

"Left turn out of the parking lot. In fact, I'm going to Regina. Follow me."

"Smart ass." Karen grinned as she walked out of the restaurant ahead of Walter and me. Walter and I drove to Regina in a comfortable silence. Sometimes I was a tiny bit jealous of the unspoken loyalty and bond Walter and Harry shared. As close as Karen and I were, it wasn't the same unconditional devotion.

We pulled into the west lot and I placed my yellow parking permit in the rear window. The alumni office had issued a permit to me since I was on campus a lot and parking was at a premium.

Walter moved to get out.

"You don't need to come with me Walter."

"Mr. Harry, he tell me to watch you good. I not able to see you from the car."

"Walter, don't worry," I assured him. "I'll be safe inside Regina's walls." The words weren't out before I gasped at what

I said. Fortunately, Walter's grasp of English didn't extend to irony. He agreed to stay in the car.

I headed for the back of Lewis Hall, toward the convent. A feeling like cold fingers on my spine settled so firmly below my neck that I had to roll my shoulders and neck to dislodge the sensation. Despite the warm air, I shivered again as I crossed the lawn.

CHAPTER ELEVEN

There seemed to be more than the usual amount of activity when I entered the building. I walked toward the east side to cut through to where the nuns lived. An ambulance was parked outside the entrance to the convent. I moved closer to a student.

"What happened?"

"Not sure. Someone said one of the nuns died. One of the old ones." Just then, I recognized one of the nuns. We had co-chaired a committee on literacy last spring. I hurried over to her.

"Sister Claire, who is it? What happened?"

"Oh, Grace, come inside. Let's get away from all these people. With the news of the 'Rosary Bride' not even a week old, another ambulance on campus brings out the curiosity seekers."

Several of the locals had come through to the campus from the nearby homes. Only a small copse of woods blocked their way. In the winter, you could see the lights of the college. Students in nearby classrooms were already spilling out into the nun's courtyard.

"Thanks, Sister. I just came by to talk to Sister Andrew."

"Oh dear, Grace. I am sorry. Sister Andrew died last night. She was, ah, found when Sister Almitas noticed that Sister was missing from morning prayers. Well, she has led a full life and now she is home with the Lord."

"I can't believe it. I just saw her a couple of days ago. We had tea together. Oh, Sister, why now? Why her?" I was near tears.

"Remember, Grace, His will be done."

I nodded meekly. "How did she die?"

"I'm not sure. Her heart, I guess. That's usually what happens when you're older. Sister Almitas said that she looked as though she were sleeping peacefully, except that her bed things were rumpled and twisted. We pray she didn't suffer too much at the end."

The finality of what Sister Claire was saying bothered me. I knew that Sister A was old, but something didn't feel right. I thanked her for asking me inside and told her that I had to leave. Once outside, I knew I didn't want to go back to the car with Walter. I wanted to go to the River Forest Police Department and talk to Ric. That was one trip I didn't want Walter reporting to Harry. I crossed through the woods to Division Street and waited on the stone bench for the Madison Street bus. While I waited, I thought about how to explain to Ric my odd feeling about Sister Andrew's death. How did I dare ask him to do an autopsy on a nun?

The bus dropped off a few blocks from the police station. I had no plan if Ric wasn't there. He looked up quickly when the front desk buzzed his office. Seated in the waiting room with the cup of coffee his secretary poured for me, I suddenly felt my reasons for being here were totally absurd.

Would Ric think them fabricated, just an excuse to meet with him? If I hadn't thought that a little myself, why did I pull that bonehead play to ditch Walter? Why was everything connected with Ric Kramer so complicated?

I had just about decided to make a break for the door,

when Ric walked toward me and motioned me to follow him to his office.

"This is a surprise Grace. A pleasure, but a surprise. Are you alone?" he asked as he looked past me to the front doors.

"Yes, I'm alone. I stopped at Regina and heard that Sister Andrew died last night. I want to talk to you about that."

"And I want to talk to you about what happened at your house last night. Karen called and told me what she knew about it. She mentioned Derek Rhodes. Do you know more about this than you told Karen?"

"No, Ric, honestly. The police think it's a break-in. Harry thinks it may have something to do with Derek. I don't know what to think."

"Could you see or hear anything about the burglar?"

"No, I was in the priest's hole."

"Lucky for you that Harry had such a Gothic side to him when you built that house. I couldn't believe it the first time I saw it in operation. You scared the hell out of me coming out of there and sneaking up on me. I almost flipped you across the room."

We were laughing at the memory his words prompted until we both remembered the rest of that afternoon. I had told Ric I would be upstairs and asked him to wait for me in the living room which is adjacent to the library. I had used the back stairs to get to the library without passing Ric. Before I hid in the priest's hole I paged him and put in Karen's number. I knew he would use the telephone in the library. That would put him at the desk with his back to the fireplace. I had removed most of my clothing in that cubby and sneaked up behind Ric with the intention of letting him remove my remaining lingerie.

Instead of romance, I had encountered military training.

He apologized repeatedly until he finally realized that I wasn't angry but that I was nearly naked. The romance that followed led to Ric's proposal that we spend our lives together. Three days later I learned that Harry was alive.

The silence strained to the breaking point.

"Why are you here, Grace, to torture me?"

"No, I think Sister Andrew was murdered."

"You think what? You must be certifiable? I'll call Madden."

His reference to the local mental health center seemed deserved. Even I hadn't called it murder before. I just had an odd feeling. In a moment of desperation, to justify my being there, I gave my intuition a name—murder!

"Grace, has the attack on you pushed you round the bend?"

"Ric, maybe not murder, I admit that's strong, but something just isn't right."

"What? What's not right? A nun in her seventies dies in her sleep from a heart attack. What's not right?"

"I don't know. I just have this feeling. Ric, you know how accurate my feelings are. I'm not some emotional incompetent!"

"Grace, I'm the first one to admit that you are intuitive and a very cool-headed lady in a crisis, but maybe the stress of this week has just, well, thrown your intuition out of whack." I realized that I did seem emotional. I sipped at my coffee and began to calmly and completely tell Ric about my visit to Sister Andrew and her comments about her trunk and Mr. Martin.

"I stopped by to see her this morning because she was going to try to write down some dates and people. Ric she was in excellent health," I continued. "She was in great shape and had just passed her physical with flying colors."

"Gracie, how could you know that?"

"She mentioned to Harry and me that she had just seen her Medicare Statement from Dr. Brusser. I happen to know that he does the nun's physicals at Oak Park Hospital."

"But how do you know she passed it?"

"Because she told us that if she hadn't been in perfect health the amount of the bill would have given her a heart attack."

I recited the last response with a smirk in my voice, like a schoolgirl who thinks she has outwitted the teacher. At the words 'heart attack', my frivolity fell away. I leaned toward Ric. "It just doesn't feel right." I hoped Ric saw the genuine concern in my eyes.

"Grace, why would anyone want to kill Sister Andrew? I'm not saying anyone did," he added quickly.

"I don't know, it doesn't make sense. I was hoping that maybe you could have someone go over and look at her room more thoroughly. Someone with an open mind. And I thought maybe I could go along to look for any information she may have left for me."

"Let me get this straight. You want a forensic team to go out to a convent and then you want permission to be at a crime scene?" The last two words told me that I had piqued his interest.

"I'll take a look myself. Then, when I tell you there's no *foul play*, will you leave it alone? The college has enough to handle without more sensationalism. Is it a deal?"

"When are we going?"

"*We're* not. I said I'd go. My way or it doesn't happen."

"But you won't know what to look for."

"Oh, excuse me. I'm such a Neanderthal that I won't recognize writing on papers, perhaps even with your name on them?"

I knew that tone. I had the major part of my request granted. I didn't push it. I did a Gemini 'about face' and smiled sweetly.

"Sure, Ric, whatever you say. Can you just drop me at Regina? I left my car there."

His eyebrows raised in advance of a question. I held up a hand.

"You don't want to know, long story."

CHAPTER TWELVE

Walter was out of the car leaning on the fender when I walked across the parking lot.

"Ma'am, I was getting worried. You was gone such long time."

"I'm sorry, Walter. It just took a little longer than I thought."

"Mr. Harry will not like so much I'm not being with you." Walter's accent thickened, as he became excited. His look of concern made me feel guilty about my shenanigans.

"Don't worry Walter, I'm fine. I will tell Mr. Harry that you did a good job."

He was not totally mollified, but he ushered me into the car and started for home. I realized that I had Mr. Martin's old address in Oak Park in my purse. I told Walter that we were going to make a stop in the area. At first he wasn't keen on letting me out of his sight again, so I promised him he could come with me.

We parked in front of 906. The four flat building had seen better days. The brick cornices were crumbling and the ivy had grown over most of the walls and two windows. One window had three broken panes giving it the appearance of an ancient game of tic tac toe. The frames, skewed from the windows, sagged and seemed ready to slide to the ground in the next strong wind.

We approached the front and rang the bell, which didn't work. Walter knocked on the screen door, then opened it, and tapped on the frosted glass with his keys. A muffled voice rewarded his efforts. The door pulled open to reveal a petite woman with fluttering movements and a shrill voice. Her small blue eyes peered out from under wisp bangs. She kept moving her hands, snatching at her hair, returning stray strands to the group. I felt as if I was looking at some strange avian species. Her hair was blondish brown and swept up in a twist that resembled a robin's nest. She fluttered her hands and ducked her head a few times as a means of greeting. I was so engrossed with her birdlike mannerisms I forgot to introduce myself.

I heard Walter apologizing for the intrusion and asking if we could speak to the 'lady of the house.' I inwardly groaned at Walter's use of such an archaic phrase and I was about to briskly introduce my business and myself when the 'bird lady' spoke.

"I am Gertrude Klops," the thin, high voice stated. She smiled at Walter and glanced sideways at me. Walter began his introduction, but halfway through he broke into his mother tongue and began waving his arms about to punctuate his conversation. A startled Gertrude Klops answered Walter in German. Two kindred spirits. They chatted easily and excitedly for several minutes before they remembered me.

"Excuse me Ma'am. I am forgotting my manners. It's just so wonderful to find someone to speak my language."

After politely shaking her hand, I asked Frau Klops if we might come in and talk to her. I discovered that Walter had told her nothing of our reason for calling. They had been discussing villages and names, trying to pin down ancestral homes and possible links.

I explained to the Frau that we were trying to find some information on Fred Martin. Her face beamed at the mention of his name. Walter looked betrayed.

"What a nice man he was. He worked for the nuns at the college. Such a nice man. He helped me here before he go to Florida. In those times my building looked nice and elegant. Nice people wanted to live here. But since Mr. Martin is gone I cannot do these things and the prices are too high to hire help."

I realized that Gertrude had been laying in wait for someone to talk to. One question unleashed an urban drama dormant these past fifteen years. Walter on the other hand was spellbound by her stories of plumbing, electrical and masonry gone bad. He clucked his tongue and ducked his head up and down in empathy. Between her fluttering and his clucking, I felt as though I were watching two lonely birds in a courting ritual. I tuned in again when Mrs. Klops mentioned Fred Martin.

"The nuns wouldn't take just nobody to be their handyman. So I knew I'd be safe to have him here. What a godsend he was." Again, Walter's pained expression. "When that other custodian was killed they needed someone very quick. Mr. Martin always said he was sorry to get his job from the tragedy on Pearl Harbor Day. But the nuns they needed a custodian, so..."

"Excuse me," I interrupted. Walter threw a look of admonishment at me for silencing his 'German Canary.' "If their custodian was at Pearl Harbor, who was doing the work anyway?"

"No, Mrs. Marsden. Karl was not at Pearl Harbor. He worked at the college."

"So who died at Pearl Harbor?"

"Oh lots of brave men, Mrs. Marsden," she replied solemnly slowly shaking her head up and down. I glanced at Walter and he was moving his head in the same solemn manner.

I felt like I had wandered into an Abbott & Costello routine. "Mrs. Klops you said that Mr. Martin felt badly that he got his job because of tragedy at Pearl Harbor."

"No, young Missus. I said because of tragedy of Pearl Harbor Day."

"Fine," I answered. I felt myself getting a little testy. "What tragedy. Who was killed at Pearl?" Walter by now was showing his open disapproval at my tone of voice.

"Karl Bauer, the custodian died Pearl Harbor Day when a statue fell on his head. Oh it was terrible. I was just a young girl, but I remember all the aunts saying how sad that a good man was taken so young. But then, lots of the good boys we knew were taken in the war and we forget about Karl Bauer."

Mrs. Klops had served coffee and cookies during the last quarter hour of this conversation. She rose from her chair and offered refills. Walter followed her to the kitchen and I heard more chatter and laughter. When they returned, Walter was beaming. Apparently, Mrs. Klops seized the occasion of a man around the house and asked Walter to 'unstuck' a window in the kitchen. She either praised his strength or his smell. My German was rusty.

At the risk of incurring Walter's wrath for once more interrupting Mrs. Klops' *stream of consciousness* renderings, I asked her about any trunks that Mr. Martin may have stored with her. An expression crossed her face like a storm cloud marching across a sunny sky.

"Ach! Those trunks!"

"Bingo!" I clapped my hands in childlike success.

"Those *verfluchen* trunks!" Her vehemence shocked Walter. "That man would do all for those nuns. He said they have no room for these important things. Nuns don't suppose to have things. They take vows to be good and poor."

Mrs. Klops was wringing her hands, plucking at strands of her hair that had come undone during her lively narrative.

I found her idea of nuns' vows very funny, but I knew she was serious and laughing now wouldn't net me any points. Instead, I calmly asked her if she still had any of the trunks.

"Sure I got them. When Mr. Martin move to Florida he tell me he will have new custodian come and take trunks away. No one ever comes. I call the school. They say they know nothing about trunks. I wrote to Mr. Martin to tell him to take these trunks out of my basement. The letters come back. Then I hear he is dead. God rest his soul."

She stopped for a breath and I jumped in. "Can we see the trunks Mrs. Klops?"

"You want to see trunks?"

"Yes, we're looking for one in particular."

"You want to see trunks, you take trunks away," came her querulous response.

"No, Mrs. Klops we don't want all of them, just one."

"You want one, you take all!"

My head was pounding from lack of sleep. I had the feeling she could be very stubborn. "How many are there?" I asked quietly.

"One whole side of basement" she answered quickly.

My heart sank when I heard her declaration. I looked at Walter for help, but he seemed to have landed squarely in her corner. Mrs. Klops had been mincing her steps towards the basement door since the first mention of those trunks. Walter preceded her to turn on the light and they both turned to look at me.

"Well, I guess we could go downstairs and take a look," I said meekly as I stood and moved toward them. Now it was Frau's turn to clap her hands. "Yawohl. At last those trunks will be gone."

I checked the nameplates on each of the twelve trunks. Walter's low voice speeding on in German with occasional pauses filled by Frau's chirping giggle sounded much different than when he spoke German to the farmer that delivered April's hay and feed every other week. They were talking too fast for me to interpret anything except tone.

"Ouch," I yelped as I rammed my shin into a corner of a trunk. I'd been eavesdropping and not paying attention to where I was walking in the crowded basement.

"Are you hurt Missus?" Walter asked as he moved towards me. "I am sorry. I can be helping you."

I felt a little guilty for breaking up their tryst, but I was more tired of cobwebs, bad lighting and barked shins. "It's okay Walter. I think I'm finished. Mrs. Klops, I'd like to take these two tonight."

"Nein, nein, " she interrupted.

"And I'll call you tomorrow and make arrangements to remove all the trunks," I finished. She smiled.

"Walter, will you please get Mrs. Klops' phone number and then we should be going?"

Walter patted his shirt pocket. "Right here is the number." Oh brother, what a fast worker.

"Thank you Mrs. Klops, I'll call you in the morning."

Walter and I carried the two lockers up the steep stairs and settled them in the back of Walter's Rover. He returned to the house for a last word with Frau Klops. I was already in the car dialing Harry when Walter got in and started up the motor.

"Damn, the batteries are too low." I pushed the cellular telephone under the seat. Karen lived just minutes away. I could call from her house and get some Advil for my headache. I gave Walter the directions. Karen lived on the top half of a brownstone. Karen and her brother had inherited quite a bit of cash when Elizabeth Kramer died. They also inherited the twelve-room house in River Forest. At that time, Ric was renting the top floor of an old brownstone in Oak Park. Neither of them wanted to maintain the big house so they sold the house and bought the brownstone. The design and remodeling required to create two separate and self-contained living units took almost six months. A lot of thought and money completed, furnished, and decorated the accommodations to suit two different lifestyles. Lights were on. I rang the bell and turned the knob at the sound of the buzzer. By the time I made it to the top of the stairs, her door was standing wide open.

"Sorry to barge in, but I need to use the phone and you're closer than..." My words faded as I realized that Karen had company. I was already halfway to the middle of her living room, making a beeline for her phone when I stopped and looked around. "I'm sorry, I didn't realize."

"It's okay Grace, really," Karen assured me graciously. "You remember my aunt and uncle don't you?"

"Of course I do. Nice to see you again." In unison, both turned smiling faces toward me. Shelly Walsh was lean and tan with angular features that reminded me of too much dieting. Her green eyes gleamed with a wolfish expression. Short, dark blonde hair framed her pointed face. Richard Walsh had close-cropped silver hair. He was medium height with a wiry build. His face seemed more lined and his complexion was definitely more sallow than hers did. His smiled appeared more genuine; it reached to his gray blue eyes.

Karen's aunt and uncle were pillars of the community and very influential, but they always reminded me of strained, taut wires like the strings on a guitar; that split second feeling right before the cat gut snaps and scares the hell out of you. I could never explain the feeling and of course would never have mentioned it to Karen. I mentioned it once to Ric and he became very protective. He accused me of not understanding the correct appearances that politically and socially connected people must assume. After that, I kept my feelings about them to myself.

"I'm here too, Grace." Ric came out from around the corner of the dining room. He was carrying a bottle of champagne and offering refills. "Can I get you a glass, Grace?"

"No thank you. I just stopped by to phone home." God, that sounded so inane. I felt like ET.

"Go right ahead. We're having a drink before we leave for the Shubert. Ric came up with last minute tickets for *Miss Saigon*."

I quickly dialed the house. Harry answered on the first ring. "Harry hi, I'm fine. I know I just lost track of time I'm sorry. No, the batteries are low. I'm calling from Karen's. Walter and I found Mr. Martin's landlady. Her name is Gertrude Klops. I've found Sister's trunk, but there are several more and I can't have one without taking all of them. It's a long story, but we're going to need a truck for tomorrow. Yes, a truck. I'm leaving now, fill you in when I get home." I turned to the room and found all eyes staring at me.

"Grace that sounds bizarre." Karen's new word for the week must be 'bizarre.'

"I know, but it's the only way I can get Sister Andrew's trunk." I glanced at Ric ready to ask about his visit to Sister's room, but he had a 'don't ask' look on his face. My glance seemed to go unnoticed as I continued my explanation.

"Walter seems smitten with her. Maybe he can change her mind tomorrow, otherwise I'm stuck with a basement full of trunks." I thanked Karen and wished them all goodnight.

"Okay Walter, let's roll." I put my hand down at my side and felt the hard outline of the cell phone on the seat. "I thought I put this away," I murmured as I pushed it out of view.

Chapter Thirteen

Between mouthfuls of a tangy shrimp salad and sips of a chilled Pinot Grigio, I told Harry the whole story of Sister Andrew's death and Mrs. Klops' trunks. He sat quietly during my entire narration, nodding at some points and smiling at my descriptions of Walter's new *squeeze*. "Remember when we were sitting with Sister A and she told us how well her physical had gone? How could those results have been so off? I think there's something wrong." I was trying to find a way to set the stage in case my visit to a certain police inspector ever became known in Pine Marsh.

"Darling, I know it's difficult for you. How close you were to her. It happens. That's probably not the answer you want. I'm more concerned with last night. I can't help think it's me that's brought this home."

I picked up the last of the dinner dishes and slipped them into the hot, sudsy water. My attempts at small talk, aimed to ease Harry's mind, proved futile. I noticed the slight tremor in his right hand when he handed me his cup. Harry waved it off as nothing for concern. I finally asked the question I'd been avoiding. "Any news on Derek?"

"No one has heard from him recently. Roger Thorpe from Kinston House seemed to think that Derek was in America."

Now I understood why he seemed so preoccupied. He blamed himself for the near miss on me.

"Do you think he came here to talk to you?"

"I don't know darling. I told him I wanted no part of them any longer. That was our agreement after South America. He knew it. They all knew it."

"Harry you wouldn't..." I left the question unfinished. Harry moved from his chair and put his arms around me. He brushed my forehead with a gentle kiss.

"Don't think about it Grace. I am a publisher now plain and simple. I know at one time, my connection to Kingston Publishing House was neither plain nor simple. That life is over. I'll never put you through that agony again."

His arms tightened around me and suddenly all I wanted was to lie down next to this safe and loving man. I fell asleep soon after our lovemaking. What should have been lovely dreams, all sweetness and light, were instead hellish dreams of the attack on Pearl Harbor. Every motion picture, newsreel, and documentary I'd ever seen on the subject must have flashed into my subconscious mind in a matter of minutes. I saw the hordes of airplanes in the sky zeroing in on the naval might of America. The ships anchored in the harbor moved gently on the water as they nodded in blissful sleep unaware of the danger from above. Flying ever closer the airborne threat became reality as each bombardier released his load to fall quickly, each bomb orienting itself to tip downward, racing toward its ultimate target. In frozen disbelief, I watched the bombs falling from the underside of the Japanese planes. I waited for my mind to replay the footage of the fire, smoke, and twisted metal that comes next. Instead, the bombs were falling on the quad at Regina College. They weren't bombs now. They were steamer trunks. One hit the ground three feet from where I stood and burst open on impact. A skeleton popped out and seemed to sway as though attached on a spring.

More trunks crashed to earth around me. Each shattered box surrendered a skeleton each a gruesome jack-in-the-box. I heard sirens, horns, whistles, and all manner of noisemakers. The loudest was a shrill ringing. A ringing that wouldn't stop. The noise was all around me.

Harry lifted the receiver and stopped the noise in my head. I felt frightened and confused by the nightmare. The clock on the nightstand read 5:00 a.m. Even *Betty Boop* looked surprised by the intrusion. Her alarm wouldn't sound for at least two more hours.

Harry listened intently and then replaced the receiver on its cradle.

"Is it about Derek," I asked slowly. The cotton stuffed feeling in my head cleared.

"No, not Derek. There has been a fire at Walter's place. That was hospital calling. The paramedics brought him in about an hour ago. Admitting found my name and number in his wallet. He's fine, but they're keeping him for observation. Touch of smoke inhalation."

"Thank God he's all right. Is he at Good Sam?"

"That's the oddity here." Harry paused. The nurse said she was calling from Oak Park Hospital. Why on earth, would they take him there? He doesn't live anywhere near Oak Park."

"No, but Mrs. Klops does. Get up, Harry. I've got a feeling the fire was in Oak Park." We were dressed and on the road in fifteen minutes. Our first stop was the hospital. Walter had been admitted. He looked a little sheepish.

"Sorry that they call you, Mr. Harry. I know is early."

"Don't be ridiculous, Walter. They were perfectly right to call. How are you old man?" Walter smiled at Harry's term of endearment.

"Ach, I am fine. I am just a little bit dizzy with all that

smoke. Poor Gertrude, ah, Mrs. Klops. Her house all full up with black smoke. Is awful bad for her."

"Walter, is Mrs. Klops all right?" I hadn't thought about her until he mentioned her name.

"Oh ya, she is fine. I make sure she get outside before I go to try and stop fire."

"You tried to put out the fire? Walter that was very dangerous."

"Ya and very stupid too!" Walter's self recrimination brought laughter from all of us. Harry and I exchanged amused glances. Walter sounded like his old self except for a hoarse voice. I stepped out to find his nurse and to him get some water or ice chips. We settled him in with apple juice and ice water and promised to check on him tomorrow. Harry pressed some folded money into Walter's hand for things he might need.

"Danke, Mr. Harry. You are good man." He certainly was that. I was thinking about Harry's generosity and sensitivity as we walked across the lot to our car. The fact that he was handsome and had a great sense of humor made him too good to be true. I smiled as I thought of the adage 'a good man is hard to find.' I grinned when I remembered the collegiate version; 'a hard man is good to find.' Harry had been both in the last few hours.

I thought of Mrs. Klops and her first impression of Walter. She must have been thanking her lucky starts. I turned to Harry with a question on my lips.

"Walter probably looks really good to Gertrude, don't you think?" Harry somehow managed to head off my thoughts and verbalized my question.

"How do you do that?"

"Druids dear, druids. When you stepped out to talk to the

nurse, Walter filled me in on the 'Frau'."

I looked at him with a certain amount of reproach.

"Sorry darling. You know Walter. He doesn't want you to think badly of Gertrude. Anyway, Walter rang Gertrude last night after you nipped up to Karen's flat to ring me. He made a date to return at nine for a late supper. They dined on pot roast and drank several beers until they were both a little tipsy. Walter claimed that Gertrude insisted that he not drive all the way home so late at night. She offered him the sofa. From this point on, Walter says that his memory is a little fuzzy. He knew he was in a deep sleep, but he thought he remembered the sound of breaking glass. The noise didn't wake him, but it did bring him closer to wakefulness. The smoke actually woke him. Walter probably saved Mrs. Klops and most of her building by his presence on the couch. Mrs. Klops' room is further from the basement stairs and she sleeps with the door closed. Gertrude can thank her lucky stars that she met the two of you yesterday." There were those stars again. Something that Harry said nagged at me, but I couldn't place it. Harry was about to continue when it hit me.

"Did you say basement stairs? Did the fire start in the basement?"

"Yes. What are you so excited about? Your eyes are positively purple!"

My peculiar eye color reacted immediately to adrenaline. Either fear or excitement turned the lavender irises speckled with gold to a deep, pansy purple.

"Harry, the basement, of course! Don't you see?"

"Frankly, no." His tone sounded flat.

"That's where the trunks are!"

Harry shrugged his shoulders slightly. "I still don't see where you're going with this."

"I do. Let's go to Mrs. Klops' building. I want to see what happened."

Harry obligingly steered the Jaguar by my directions until we pulled up in front of 906 Cedar Street. The fire trucks were gone, but evidence of the fire was apparent everywhere. The side of the building directly above the basement was covered with fire marks and soot. All the windows on that side, including the basement windows were broken out; efforts of the firefighters to enter the house and contain the fire.

Telltale yellow police tape prohibited access to the east-side. On closer inspection, the damage seemed contained on that side. We hadn't gone in yet. As we approached the front steps, we nearly collided with Mrs. Klops. She was walking with her head bent down talking earnestly with a man in a fire department uniform.

She looked up and smiled slightly as she recognized me. She thanked the fire investigator and turned to greet us. I introduced Harry to her and Gertrude was immediately charmed with my dear Harry.

"We've just been to see Walter. He's doing fine," Harry assured her. Tears welled up in her eyes at the mention of his name.

"Ach, what a brave man! He make sure everybody get outside of house and that we was safe. I'm feeling so bad that he is sick with the smoke. I told him don't go back no more."

I gently caught one of her fluttering hands and quietly told her, "It wasn't your fault Gertrude, let's go inside."

"Walter says that you are nice lady. He is right."

She invited us in. Gertrude proceeded to extol Walter's bravery. In an effort to get back on track, I asked her if we might look at the basement. She nodded yes.

As we descended the steep, rickety stairs, I marveled at

how, at nighttime, these old basements always reminded me of scary places. I grew up in an old house in the city's Italian neighborhood around Taylor and Ashland. The basement was used for laundry and storage by my parents and roach hunting by my older brothers. The deal I had with the imagined monsters in my basement was that if I could go down and back within a certain number count that I declared on the landing, they couldn't come out and grab me. Another manifestation of obsessive compulsive behavior. At the time, I thought it the safest way to obey my mother when told to bring up an item and still elude the ghoulies' grasp.

"Looks like 100 to me," I muttered under my breath.

"Say again?"

"Nothing. Just thinking out loud." I pulled out a deep purple length of yarn and started down the stairs.

The sun was just coming up and with the windows broken out, there would be enough light streaming into the basement in a few minutes to make everything quite visible. Most of the fire damage was concentrated on the outside wall. The trunks were lined up two deep against the adjacent wall. Every surface was covered with soot and water. What an awful mess for Gertrude. I was wondered if she had kept her homeowners insurance up-to-date. A small grunt from Harry, who had walked to the other side of the basement, got my attention.

"What's that?" I pointed to a huge octopus type metal structure.

"That, my dear, is where a fire in the basement of an old run-down house normally starts. He accented normally. Harry made the connection I had leaped to earlier. In all fairness to Harry's sleuthing abilities, I hadn't had a chance to tell him my suspicion about Sister Andrew's death.

"Someone didn't want you having a look-see at those

trunks darling. That's why the fire started at that end of room where there is nothing combustible and not at this end of the room in an old furnace."

"That's not all." I quickly filled him in on Sister A.

Harry nodded his head in agreement with my suspicions. It seemed that people and property connected with the 'Rosary Bride' were starting to disappear. Harry went out to the car and used the phone.

"Done and done," Harry announced when he returned to the kitchen. "A truck will be here within the hour to remove the trunks. The driver can deliver the remaining trunks to Regina. I have already cleared storage with Sister Joan."

"How in heaven's name did you do that?

"I convinced her to take delivery with a vague line about private papers, college memorabilia almost destroyed, and Providence stepping in, etc.," was his blithe response.

I was always amazed at whom my husband knew and how quickly and easily people did things for him. I followed him meekly down the stairs forgetting to assign a count to this trip.

He found an old screwdriver to assist his attempts at breaking the lock on the trunk furthest from the wall. Harry turned the strong beam from the borrowed flashlight on the writing.

"Apparently Mr. Martin was the soul of organization," I commented as we started reading the nametags. "He had marked each trunk with the college name and the nun's name. His attention to detail certainly made it easy for me to find those two trunks last night. We want anything else marked Sister Andrew."

Since we had only one flashlight, we worked together. I swung the light on trunk number five, when the beam of light dimmed and then went out.

"The bloody torch is done for." Harry sounded annoyed.

"I'll see if there's one in the car." As I emerged from the basement, I realized how smoky the air was down there. It was so fresh by contrast up in the kitchen. I started for the door when I heard a familiar voice. Karen Kramer was asking Mrs. Klops if she could come in. I turned the corner as Karen explained who she was. She spotted me and broke off her explanation.

"What are you doing here?" I asked.

"I've been calling your house all morning. I remembered you said you were going to move the trunks and here I am. Deducing must run in the family," she finished. Karen's eyes sparkled like polished agates.

"Nice work Miss Marple, but how did you know where I was?"

"You mentioned Mrs. Klops name last night, so I just let my fingers do the walking."

"Since you're here, you might as well help. Harry is downstairs, through the kitchen and left." As Karen moved to follow my direction, I turned to Gertrude.

"We've arranged for a truck to be here soon to remove those trunks. It will be easier to clean up and repair the walls with them out of the way." What I neglected to say was that she'd be safer if those trunks weren't in her house or her life.

CHAPTER FOURTEEN

As I rummaged through the emergency kit in the trunk, I heard car tires coming up fast behind me. I turned and froze, certain of the bone-crushing impact. The scream forming in my lungs stopped abruptly as the car racing toward me screeched to a stop two short feet away. Something snapped when I realized that Ric was the driver.

"Are you crazy, you could have killed me!"

Ric looked genuinely astonished that I was so enraged.

"Gracie, calm down. I didn't even come close." He put his hand out to touch my cheek.

"Don't touch me!" I hissed. Harry, Karen, and Mrs. Klops rushed from the house in time to hear me ranting at Ric. I knew I was out of control but I couldn't stop. The events of the last twenty-four hours had finally taken their toll.

"Gracie, what's the matter?" Harry reached us first and put his arm around my shoulders. "Kramer, what's this about?"

"Damned if I know. I pulled up and before I could say hello she just came unglued!"

Ric's calm scenario infuriated me even more.

"Pulled up! Is that what you call screeching to a halt inches away from a person. You could have killed me," I repeated with a catch in my throat. Harry's eyebrow raised slightly almost imperceptibly. I couldn't read the exchange of glances between him and Ric.

"Look Grace, I'm sorry if I scared—"

"Forget it!'

"Grace, come on," Ric pleaded.

"I said forget it!' I whirled on my heel and moved toward the house. As I neared Karen, she turned to follow me. My hysteria with Ric no doubt upset her. She had learned in the years since Harry's return that Ric and I always seemed a heartbeat away from destroying each other's mental health.

"I only came by to tell you that we're labeling the nun's death suspicious and opening an investigation." His voice stopped me. I turned and slowly retraced my steps to stand directly in front of him.

"You did an autopsy?"

"No, not yet. I've ordered a hold on the body. When I examined Sister Andrew's room, I noticed an afghan on her bed. It was crumpled up not smooth as though she used it to cover herself."

"Sister Claire said that they noticed that her bed linens were rumpled and twisted. They hoped that she hadn't writhed in pain unable to call out for help."

"I know. I spoke to Sister Claire. She also told me that Sister A always had that afghan draped over her reading chair more as a decoration than as a blanket. Anyway, I bagged the afghan and sent it to the lab. Something just didn't feel right."

"What made you suspicious?" Harry's question boomed in my ears. An obvious question. An insensitive answer could do so much damage.

Facing Ric as I was, only he could see the anguish in my eyes. Would he keep my visit to him in confidence? Or, would he deliver another blow to a relationship he'd like to see ended. The hired truck arrived as Ric was about to answer. Question forgotten, we hurried to point out what to load.

Karen and I armed with our new flashlight, squeezed between the remaining trunks to find Sister Andrew's. In the end, we found only one trunk. The nametag read Sister A.

Ever logical Karen suggested, "Since there's only one trunk and no one has a vehicle big enough to carry it, let the driver deliver all the trunks to Regina and we can sort it out tomorrow."

It was at this point that Ric pulled rank. He announced his intention to impound the trunks as possible evidence in a suspicious death. Karen and I protested, but Ric ignored us and called for a police van. Harry held up a piece of paper.

"What's that Marsden?"

"A bill of sale from Mrs. Klops for those trunks."

A stunned silence filled the room.

"Harry when on earth—" I started to ask, but was interrupted by an angry detective.

"What are you trying to pull? I told you these trunks could be evidence."

"And I told you that these trunks are my property," he turned to me in explanation and continued, "which I duly purchased earlier."

"I don't care what you *duly* purchased. This arson investigation may be connected to a homicide. Sorry, *old man*," Ric sarcastically used that term, "but your receipt isn't worth the paper it's written on." The two men glared at each other. This time I fully understood the looks they exchanged.

Gertrude had been more than patient about our presence in her basement all day. The laborer from the company she hired to board up the windows worked around us. The insurance investigator had insisted that we wait for her to complete her investigation regardless of which trunks we were searching for.

I was impressed with the investigator's speed and

efficiency. Sherry Adams from Great States Insurance had lost no time in checking out the area. She immediately pinpointed the cause and origin of the fire and pointed that out to Ric. They weren't keeping their voices low. It was easy to follow their conversation.

"The odd thing about this arson, Inspector is that the perpetrator didn't bring anything with them."

"What do mean?" Ric asked.

"They relied on the usual basement clutter and a fortuitous can of charcoal lighter. Amateurish. You can see where the splash pattern ran its course too soon to ignite everything that was propped up against the trunks. Probably wasn't a full can of liquid."

"That makes no sense. Unless it wasn't a premeditated arson?" Ric looked puzzled.

"Or," Ms. Adams added, "the arsonist knew there were materials on hand."

I felt a tightening in my throat, as Gertrude was again questioned by the fire department. This time a policewoman sat with them.

Ric finished with the investigator just as two officers arrived to assist him. He must have known he was going to impound the trunks. Karen and I watched helplessly as the Sister A trunk was loaded on the truck. Karen was furious. "I can't believe how unreasonable Ric is being," she fumed. "He would never have even known about the trunks if it weren't for you. It doesn't seem fair that we don't get to look inside."

"If he thinks these trunks can mean anything to his investigation, I guess he has to take them," I answered.

"You're pretty calm about all this, I don't get it. The one trunk that might give us some answers and you stand there defending him." Karen shook her head and shrugged.

"I know, I was upset at first, but the trunk marked Sister A isn't going to help us. Sister A is a recent nickname. That's probably a more recent trunk than the one we want."

"Grace, that is absolutely brilliant," gushed Karen.

"And anyway," I continued, "last night, Walter and I loaded two trunks into his Rover. One is marked Sister Andrew and the other K. Bauer."

"The handyman? Why would you want his trunk?" questioned Karen.

"I don't know. It was getting late, I had her trunk, and I just thought I'd like to see what was in his. His name keeps coming up. Anyway it was close to the stairs and I thought I'd be getting any other trunks I wanted today."

"You devil," teased Karen. "My brother would spit if he knew you had those trunks. This is great. That'll teach 'Mr. High and Mighty' a lesson. I love it. I've gotta' go. I was supposed to meet my aunt twenty minutes ago." She rushed off mumbling about River Forest being filled with old trunks.

After Harry explained to his hired driver why the police were loading up his truck and a police van with the trunks and why his destination was the police station and not the college, he went inside to call Sister Joan at Regina to cancel the delivery. Ric and I stood silently looking at nothing and everything, trying to avoid looking at each other. He stepped closer to me.

"What the hell was that all about earlier. You know I didn't even come close to hitting you. You know I wouldn't hurt you, couldn't hurt you, don't you?"

"I know." My reply was a whisper.

"What then?"

"I don't know, I just felt threatened, I..." I felt the flush start around my throat and move up to my cheeks. He moved one step closer. I looked up and knew that my eyes were darkening like the night sky when clouds cover the moon.

"Are you scared now, Gracie?" Ric asked as he placed two fingers under my chin. I shook my head and immediately regretted answering him.

"Good. Then you must be excited." He tapped the bottom of my chin to underscore his observation. He smiled smugly, turned, and walked up the stairs.

I was furious with the way I still felt about him and the way my body had betrayed me. My lower lip trembled. 'Oh, God. I'm going to cry,' I thought. Instead, a smile started to replace the quiver as I realized that Harry and I would have the last laugh on 'Mr. High and Mighty' as Karen called him. We waited for the truck, the police, and Ric to leave. Harry draped his arm around my shoulders as we watched them go.

"Darling, since you don't drive stick, you'd best drive Walter's Rover," his eyes sparkled with amusement. "We're certainly fortunate that the Inspector didn't ask about any other trunks."

"Harry, you did that whole bill of sale thing on purpose, didn't you?"

"I knew he'd take the trunks if he thought they were connected to a crime. I only hoped that my attempt at interference would keep him concentrating only on the trunks in the basement."

"You are brilliant," I hugged him. Harry kissed me and turned me toward the Land Rover.

"You lead."

We separated and started our engines. I appreciated the solitude on the way home. I should have been thinking about the trunks. Instead, my thoughts centered on the two men who loved me and whom I loved. How easily could love turn to hurt, to humiliation, to hate?

* * *

The drive home was quick and not nearly enough time to settle anything in my head let alone my heart. I was approaching 'the pass,' our nickname for the narrow lane entrance to Pine Marsh when Harry flashed his high beam.

I waved to him as he passed me. He probably went ahead to open the gate to our property and make room in the garage. I heard the Jag shifting gears and just then lost the pinpoints of his taillights.

Our house was one of six in a beautiful piece of DuPage County called Pine Marsh. Since the area was still mainly marshland, locals referred to the community as The Marsh. At least they didn't call it 'the swamp.' Natural barriers and two electronic gates prevented uninvited guests from dropping in, and passersby from snooping. That was if they were driving. If they were on foot, they could walk across the marsh from many points. The developers put in several running paths and trails without spoiling the natural landscape.

I noticed a car behind me and wondered which neighbor was coming home. It turned with me as I came off the paved road and onto one of the gravel lanes that divided the entrances to Pine Marsh. I didn't recognize the car, but it must be a neighbor. No one else, unless they were lost, would turn here. Just beyond the bridge the lane ended at a crossroads. The Trotters, Rowes, and Clarks entered from the left side while Harry and I, the Bishops, and the Atwaters entered our properties from the right lane. *I'll know who this is as soon as we cross the marsh,* I thought.

The bridge at the entrance to the lanes really was necessary. The other bridges, seven in all, were considered more decorative than functional. Those were wooden and not made to withstand more than bicycles or golf carts.

The main bridge was steel but covered in wood to maintain the ambiance. This bridge spanned the deepest part of the marsh, which was quite untenable even on foot. Surveyors told us there were sinkholes and other dangers and they warned us about letting our pets stray this far from the developed areas.

Suddenly, I heard an engine roar. The car behind me picked up speed. I saw the left headlight first and then the right one as the car moved out into the lane.

"Okay pass me," I muttered. The car pulled even with me and then began to move ahead. Just before the bridge, the car abruptly swerved into my path. Instinctively I slammed on the brakes and jerked the wheel to the right. I realized too late that the shoulder near the bridge was narrow and melted immediately into a sloping embankment. The Rover started to slide to the right. It felt as though the top was pitching toward the marsh, about to roll end over end to the bottom. I screamed and tried to hold on to the wheel, to ride out the crash. I heard frantic beeping and then squealing tires as a car sped away. The twisting, bruising ride I was braced for never came. I realized that after the initial lurch sideways and back, the Rover hadn't moved. The car wasn't level; without lifting my head I could see the stars. I undid my seat belt and tried to sit up. The car moved a little. I froze. I heard running feet.

"Are you all right?" A breathless Harry appeared at my window, well sort of at my window, but at a strange angle. I shifted my weight to face him. The car slid.

"Don't move Grace. God, don't move." The strain in his voice scared me.

"Harry," one word; a volume of meaning.

"Don't worry. I'll get you out. Just don't move around." It seemed forever, but soon Harry was in my sight again.

"Is the driver's door locked?"

"Yes."

"All right listen to me. Can you reach the button and unlock it?"

"Yes."

"All right then do it, but move as little as possible."

I stretched my arm forward and began inching my fingers forward. Because of the angle, I couldn't reach it without leaning forward. I told Harry.

"Gracie, wait. Let me explain what you have to do. I've used the jumper cables to secure your bumper to the bridge. I don't know how much weight they can take. The ground under the tires is soft. You can't stay in there much longer. This ground is likely to go any minute. Look for the door lever. When you move to unlock the door, push the lever and move against the door all in one motion. You're tipped back so you've got to come up and out in one motion. Do you understand Gracie, one movement?"

I understood exactly what Harry was telling me. In short, I had one chance to get out of this thing or take my chances rolling into the marsh.

I tried to calm myself and pull every fiber of a very jittery being together to make this effort work. 'Oh, no. Not now.' The compulsive creature that lives in my mind was starting to raise its disruptive head. I needed to find my yarn and braid ten loops before I could open the door. That voice in my head, that monster that lived in me was choosing now to take hold of me. "Nooo," I whimpered.

"Gracie, don't be scared. You can do this. Hurry, darling. You can't wait." Harry pleaded.

I had to braid but if I moved to pull the yarn from my back pocket, I might send the truck into the muck below.

"Oh, Grace. Not now." Harry finally understood.

I sat frozen willing myself not to reach for my 'lifeline.' I heard, since I couldn't see him from my angle, Harry patting his pockets searching for something. I heard scraping on the ground.

"Here, Gracie. Hurry." A white shoelace from his running shoes landed gently in my lap. One plastic tip touched my right thumb.

I could do this now, in my lap, without moving. The voice in my head said 'fifty loops.' 'No,' I argued. 'Ten was the deal.' My mind agreed as I completed the second loop.

"Grace, talk to me. How many? Where are you?"

"Ten," I said. "Only ten. Done." My fingers stopped their fury.

"That's a good girl. Ready now. Remember, it has to be all one movement." Harry's voice washed over me. I felt ready.

The door handle was closer to my left hand than the button. They were both on the door panel but inches apart. Thank God the car was still running. Electric buttons wouldn't do me any good if the engine had stalled. If I reached across with my right hand to release the lock and pulled the handle with my left, I could push with my left shoulder and hopefully, roll out onto the ground, but not under the car if it started to go. Still, at this moment being out of the car seemed safer than being in it.

"Okay. One, two, three." I reached, pulled, and pushed with as much of one motion as I could muster. The lock clicked, the door handle opened leaving my left arm, shoulder, and my head clear of the door. My momentum slowed as the angle of the car and gravity began to work against me. The door swung back on its hinges pinning me. I managed to swing my left foot out, and I felt the door slam back against my shin.

A wave of pain swept over me as I screamed for Harry. I felt him tug at my shoulder trying to get a good hold. The Rover strained and then I heard a plastic 'snap' as the cables let go. Still more inside the car than out, I felt the muddy slope give way as the car slid slowly toward the marsh threatening to drag me down into its murky depths.

CHAPTER FIFTEEN

Harry held on. Terrified that he'd be pulled down with me, I yelled at him to let go. Increased pressure on my shoulder was his response. If I didn't get out, Harry wasn't going to let go. I heaved against the door with a strength I didn't know I possessed. The vehicle's forward momentum pushed the door open enough that Harry could grab my right wrist and pull me out. The Rover started to slide away as I plunged two feet onto the gravel. Harry was still clutching both of my arms; the victor in a deadly tug-of-war. I rolled closer into him and watched in horror as the Rover slowly gained speed, tumbled, turned, and stopped inches from the marsh. It came to rest on its roof with the rear wheels still spinning. I huddled motionless in Harry's arms.

Officer Peterson's bulk filled one of the wooden chairs in my kitchen. He was asking questions about the second attempt on my life in as many days. The questions were the same; so were the answers.

"I told you, I couldn't recognize the person in the other car."

Harry was no help. He had seen the whole thing in his rear view mirror, freezing with terror as a glance in the mirror showed him two sets of headlights jockeying for position across the too narrow road. Our neighbor, Barb Atwater, had been walking over the bridge out of Pine Marsh during the final moments of the drama and called 911 from her cell phone. She had heard only the whine of an engine shifting gears and moving quickly.

"This was no accident, Peterson. When I turned back to the bridge, the other car had stopped, but not to help. It was coming back to finish the job. I jammed on the accelerator and began sounding the horn to scare him off. I never got close enough to see the driver."

Officer Peterson nodded as he entered his last notes in his book. "Lucky for you Mrs. Marsden that your husband was close by again." I'll get this report together and have someone call you in the morning. I need you to come in and sign a statement. Mr. Marsden, I am assigning another officer to the compound patrol."

The compound patrol was a private security service that worked closely with the police. Pine Marsh was very exclusive and very expensive. Officer Peterson was trying to assure us that his department would cover all bases. Harry had made a few arrangements of his own after calling the police. He called in a favor and a large and rather serious friend named Max would be on our doorstep tomorrow morning like the Sunday Tribune.

The next morning Max sat at our kitchen table with the paper spread out across four square feet of oak. He skimmed each column like an Evelyn Wood honors student. A carafe of coffee, rasher of bacon and plate of firmly scrambled eggs covered the remainder of the table.

I carried breakfast, for Harry and me, on a tray into his office. Harry was placing calls to London waking up friends with a mildly apologetic tone.

"Sorry to wake you, Holling. It's Harry Marsden. I need you to find Derek. It is urgent, or I wouldn't ring you."

I munched on toast and sipped coffee while Harry finished his calls.

"Darling, I've done all I can for the moment. I'm going to drive in and pick up Walter from hospital. You'll be safe with Max."

"Don't worry, I've some galleys to occupy me. Give my love to Walter."

Harry held both of my hands up to his lips and placed a gentle kiss on each palm. He closed them in a prayer position and covered them with his hands. "I won't let anything happen to you."

My eyes misted over and I just nodded my head not trusting my voice to speak. After watching him leave I filled the coffee butler and settled down with galleys, coffee, and marker. Just as I had everything positioned, the doorbell rang. I motioned Max back to the kitchen and opened the door. A very annoyed Ric Kramer was on my doorstep.

"Do I have to hear about this from a stranger, Grace?"

"And exactly why is *anyone* calling you about me?" My question sounded as terse as his did.

"Because I've flagged your file. Anything that pertains to you and Marsden is forwarded to me. My file on you is growing and I want to know why!"

The coffee I intended on offering him just about ended up in his face. Controlling my temper was always hard work.

"Stop trying to insinuate yourself back into my life by hinting that Harry and I are hiding something."

"Not you, Grace, but Harry."

"I knew you'd get around to—" I started to say.

Max quietly moved to stand in the doorway when he heard

the anger in my raised voice.

"Ric Kramer, this is Max uh, Max. He's staying with us for a few days. Max, this is Inspector Kramer."

Max nodded a greeting and unfolded his arms to extend a handshake that covered Ric's entire hand. I thought of the child's game of scissors, paper, rock, and wanted to giggle.

"Grace, let's take this outside."

"Here," I handed him the coffee butler. "We can sit on the patio." We settled ourselves on chairs opposite each other.

"Now listen to me. Every time something happens, Harry is in on it." He waited until I filled our coffee cups with steaming caffeine and until my hands were folded motionless atop the table before he continued.

"Someone shoots at you. Harry's not home, but he's conveniently around the corner. Someone drives you off the road. Harry's just out of sight across the bridge. You tell Harry about the trunks and a fire is set. You both see Sister A and then she's murdered"

My eyes widened at the word *murdered*. Ric saw it.

"Yes. I got the autopsy report. She was smothered with her pillow. The ME found traces of her saliva and denture cream on the pillowcase. Housekeeping says that the pillowcase had been changed that afternoon." Before I could comment, he continued.

"We found the gun that was used in the break-in. Some kids found it down at the marsh. Want to guess who owns the gun? It's registered to Harry Marsden."

"Ric, you know his gun was stolen. He reported it missing two weeks ago."

"How convenient," was his caustic reply. "Now we meet Mrs. Klops. A nice lady who never had any trouble until 'Nick and Nora' pay her a visit. Bingo. Arson. And last night you were run off the road by a car that came out of nowhere and left the same way according to our only eyewitness," Ric paused, "your husband." The last word dripped with innuendo.

"How dare you take pot shots at Harry. What on earth is wrong with you? Are you so jealous that you'd stoop to trumping up a case against him? This whole thing started with the 'Rosary Bride'. Are you going to accuse Harry of that too?" I knew my face flushed red and that my eyes were deepening to black. Hot tears of anger filled my eyes, threatening to spill over.

"Gracie, listen to me. Ever since we've seen each other again, strange things have been happening. The *bride* has nothing to do with those things. She just brought us together. Grace, I think Harry is having trouble again."

The pronouncement came with such calm and clarity that for a brief moment I was ready to believe him. Just as quickly the moment passed and I knew that I must defend Harry and stop this accusation before anyone else heard it.

"No Ric you're wrong, desperately wrong."

"I know you don't want to hear it Grace, but the pattern is there. Remember how he went berserk when he first found out about us. He was wild. He raved about a conspiracy. He threatened you, me and even Karen for her part in our involvement."

"Stop it. Don't ever repeat that. Do you hear me? Harry went through hell once because of us and I won't let you do it again!" We were both on our feet and I was shouting at this point frantic to make him understand.

"Okay, Grace, okay take it easy."

I pushed his hand away. "Don't tell me to take it easy. Do you think I'd run to you again if he were out of the picture?"

Ric stepped back as though slapped. Minutes of silence

seemed to pass as I struggled to regain my composure. I had to be firm. This kind of talk wasn't going past this moment in time. Harry had struggled to regain and protect his privacy after his rescue. I wouldn't allow misplaced love to destroy that trust.

"I don't mean to be so hard on you. I'm sorry. I've been up for almost two days. We never did make it to the theater that night," Ric explained. Karen was really upset—"

"Karen," I interrupted. "I promised her that we'd look through, I mean that I'd call her today," I stammered. Ric, excuse me, I'll be right back."

"I know about the trunks," he said softly, stopping me in my tracks. "That's the other reason I'm here. You and your husband are skating very close to the 'impeding a criminal investigation' line."

"Walter and I loaded them the night before and well, I guess I just forgot they were in there until I had to drive..." I stopped lamely. "How did you know?"

"Mrs. Klops made an offhand remark to one of the officers about the total number of trunks. My officer finally decided it might be important that the count was short by two trunks. He called me this morning."

"Let's just you and me look in them now. Please, Ric? I mean what difference does it make if we look inside now or you take them back and open them?" I was banking on the fact that Ric wanted to be the good guy for me and that he'd say yes. It was a crummy ace up my sleeve to play and I regretted the ploy as soon as I used it. Ric liked the idea of *us* doing something together.

"Okay, Gracie girl, you've got yourself a deal," he smiled broadly.

"Ah, Ric, I can't, I mean, we can't open them without

Karen. I promised her last night she could be here. I have to call her; she's probably waiting for the call. I'll be right back." Ric's face reflected his disappointment.

I used the cellular phone on the patio to dial Karen's number. "Hello," an unfamiliar voice answered.

"May I speak with Karen please," I asked, half expecting the voice to tell me I had the wrong number. Instead, I heard, "one moment please" and then "Hello, this is Karen."

"Hi Karen. It's Grace. Do you have company?"

"No, I'm the company. I'm at my aunt's house so I had my calls forwarded. What's up?"

"I thought you'd like to be around when Ric and I opened the trunks." I purposely made my voice sound offhand and casual.

"When Ric and you," a pause, "sure kiddo. When does Geraldo turn the key?"

The phone clicked.

"Hold on Karen, I've someone on the line."

"Hello."

"Hello, darling. I'm on the way to Walter's place. I have to stop at the pharmacy for him, but then I'll be along. Poor devil still has an awful headache."

"I've Karen on the line. I asked her to come out and rummage through the trunks with me. Ah, Ric is here now, he knows about the trunks, and he wants to be present when we open the trunks in case of evidence I guess."

I tried to fill the silence with more explanations; it was going badly.

"Shall I ring before I arrive?" was Harry's sarcastic query. The line went dead.

"Karen?"

"Grace, I'd love to come out, but I took my car to the shop

this morning. Some jerk smashed into it while it was parked on the street last night. You won't believe the estimate. I walked over to my aunt's house.

"No problem," feeling a wave of buoyancy. "I'll send Ric for you. See you in about two hours."

This would give me a chance to talk to Harry alone. Just then, Max asked if he could use the phone. He was looking down at the display on his pager. Hi-tech muscle. He replaced the receiver and started for the door.

"Max, where are you going?"

"That was Mr. Marsden. He told me I could leave since the police are here with you."

"Wait a minute. Mr. Marsden paged you?"

"Yes Ma'am. He said he'd be home soon and that the Inspector would stay with you."

While Max took his leave by the front door Ric walked in from the patio. He moved through the kitchen with the practiced ease of someone who was very familiar with the territory. That bothered me. Today, everything bothered me. Now Harry was playing games. I knew he had released Max from his post so I would be alone with Ric. Both of these guys were really ticking me off today.

I gave Ric the plan. He wasn't thrilled at the prospect of the drive, but I think he knew it was better this way. Ric and Karen together were less threatening. Ric walked me out to the carriage house. "Oh, here Grace, this is yours." Ric handed me my yellow parking permit for Regina. "I found it on Mrs. Klops' lawn," he explained. "You must have dropped it yesterday."

"Thank you. They get testy if we don't have one." We reached the carriage house. "Hey, one trunk is already open. You were supposed to wait for me." I admonished.

"Sorry, I couldn't wait any longer. I can't believe all the stuff Sister A kept in here." Ric lowered the lid and wiped the dust from his hands. "I'm grateful that you didn't roll into that marsh, but I'm also grateful that the Rover stopped short of going under. It would have taken days to dry out everything."

"Hurry up and go get Karen. I'm making coffee and sandwiches. On your way out, ask *Officer Surveillance* if he'd like some?"

"It must be nice to have private muscle and local police power. I'll let Pine Marsh's elite know you're cooking for the men in uniform," he quipped. For the first time that day, a smile came easy to both of us. Ric gave me a mock salute as he left through the side door. He stopped and turned, and suddenly he was a serious fellow again. "I'm scheduling a police van to pick up the trunks tomorrow. That's how it has to be."

"I know. Thanks for the chance to look inside."

My promise of coffee and sandwiches in my head, I turned to go back to the house. The unlocked trunk proved too much of a temptation. I decided to rummage until Harry came home. I checked my watch. Time enough later to prepare lunch.

CHAPTER SIXTEEN

A voice from behind the rose hedge called my name. My neighbor Barb Atwater followed her salutation around the floral corner.

"Good morning," she started. "I came by to see how you were feeling." Barb Atwater approached the carriage house with a smile and a saran wrapped pan. "I didn't want to call too early; thought those bruises might have kept you in bed longer today."

"Good morning. I was too restless to sleep. My muscles certainly know I did something different with them, they don't approve." I motioned toward the patio. "I have coffee. Looks like you brought the 'and,'" I said and motioned toward the pan.

Barb smiled and nodded. "Yep. Fresh from the oven, cinnamon twists." She handed me the pan. "I hid some before Devin could eat them all."

Devin was Barb's seventeen-year-old, six foot, two inch son, who never met a meal he didn't like. He was dark haired like Barb, but he had his father's genetic footprint in every other way. Devin was good-natured and often helped Harry with some of the manual labor required to get the gardens prepared in the spring.

"I hope you're not depriving that boy," I teased.

"That'll be the day. Look at what he's got me doing for him now." Barb pulled a small tape recorder and a folded paper from the pocket in her windbreaker. "Since I walk the back woods every morning, Devin decided I could be a spotter." I must have looked perplexed. She hurried to explain. "Several sections of the woods run parallel to the golf course, holes four, eight, twelve, thirteen and seventeen, I think." She unfolded the paper. A grid pattern covered the sheet. Neatly drawn numbers filled in the grid at spaced intervals. "My job, should I choose to accept it," she paraphrased the opening line from Mission Impossible, (the Peter Graves version), "is to verbally note in accordance with his map where I spot golf balls.

"Golf balls?" I shrugged my shoulders.

"Devin has a new idea on how to make money."

"What? He doesn't like schlepping composted manure and digging up gardens twice a season?" I asked.

"Oh, he loves that. Says it keeps him in shape. Harry is a generous employer. Like you said, it's only twice a season. With this plan, he can make money from spring through fall. After I give him the location, he can go out and collect the balls. He's going to recondition them and sell them as *only driven once.*"

"What a great idea. Let me know when he's open for business. I've lost quite a few off those tees, especially in the water on seven."

"He's got that covered too," Barb explained. "He got permission to collect the balls from the water hazards too. Devin is a certified diver for shallow dives. I think they call them puddle divers." Barb beamed whenever she spoke of her son. She refolded and pocketed her map. "If this business is going to start, I'd best get walking."

"What about your coffee?" I asked.

"No thanks. I just wanted to stop by and see how you

were feeling, and bring those for you and Harry." She put a hand on my arm. "That was so scary last night, seeing Harry struggling to hold you. I almost screamed when the cable snapped." She squeezed my arm and turned to retrace her steps. She stopped at the hedge, her bright blue windbreaker a sharp contrast to the cotton candy pink roses. "I know you're a morning person. Why don't you join me some morning?"

"Maybe I will. Bye."

Barb waved and disappeared behind the roses. Maybe I would start walking with her. I could use the exercise. I put down the goodies on the table and walked back to the carriage house. A quick peek at my watch assured me that I'd only spent ten minutes with Barb. I still had time to rummage.

The heavy lid resisted at first, but then lifted easily. The trunk teemed with leather bound books, portfolios, and loose-leaf journals. The contents represented the collective opinion and essence of Sister Andrew. A twinge of guilt almost stayed my twitching fingers. My hands carefully lifted out a folder of deep turquoise with delicate copper colored paisley. The journal reflected her involvement with programs at the college concerning Vatican II. Interesting, but not the brass ring I anticipated.

Another journal, a deep ruby hue with a black border, surrendered its secrets. I glanced at my watch. Over an hour had passed and Harry still wasn't home. I needed a break. The air in the carriage house seemed warm and smothering. I folded the journal and stuffed it in my back pocket, planning to read it in the kitchen while I prepared lunch. Harry, no doubt was driving around taking some time to come to grips with his feelings. The cloying, stale air made my head throb. Disjointed thoughts stumbled through my brain and scattered before I could take hold of their meaning.

It's stuffy in here. Maybe Harry thinks I want to be with Ric. He knows Karen is coming out. He knows it takes an hour. Sandwiches don't take an hour. Maybe he's waiting to see her car, so he won't cause a scene. A paisley scene. Maybe he knows how hot it is. He's not coming home until I open the door. 'Open the door so Harry comes home, open the door so Harry comes home. Chanting, sweating, standing and then swirling, putting my hands out to stop the concrete.

I became aware of the sudden swaying and staccato siren as my mind cleared somewhat. Harry held my hand, leaning forward, looking anxiously into my face. When I opened my eyes and wriggled my fingers in a greeting, his face beamed with relief. I couldn't see him clearly around the oxygen mask. He smiled and kissed my forehead, but I wanted to squeeze his hand. It seemed like too much of an effort. I closed my eyes and my mind glided away from the garish light of day and back to a quiet inky-dark place. I was floating. Sometimes I heard Harry calling my name. He was so far away. I kept floating.

When I opened my eyes again, I was told it was the next day. Apparently, carbon monoxide poisoning victims aren't okay just because they're still breathing when they're found. There are calculations (how long vs. how much vs. lung tolerance.) The possibility of complications for the first twenty-four hours accounted for the guarded prognosis. The nurse that explained all this to me also informed me that while I had floated between almost awake and soundly asleep, Harry, all available Morellis, and Karen had kept vigil through the night and into the next afternoon. Ric had been there too. I finally stopped floating, rooted to my hospital bed, and opened my eyes. I looked up at my brother Joseph.

"I hope you're not here on business," I said in a voice that was little more than a whisper. My throat burned dry and hot. My lips felt fuller than Kim Bassinger's looked. Joseph smiled and squeezed my hand. In a matter of seconds, they were all in my room smiling, crying, hugging, and kissing. The nurses, after what they considered a generous amount of time, shagged them out except for Harry. In the next few moments we said all the things to each other that you say when you thought you wouldn't get a chance to say them.

Asking 'what happened' seemed trite, but that was what I wanted to know.

Harry filled me in. "I was furious after I rang off with you. I dropped Walter at home and stopped at the chemist. I went driving, trying to sort out my feelings. I knew Karen would be there in about an hour; I timed my arrival to coincide with hers. I pulled up, but didn't see her car, or Ric's. I assumed that Ric had pulled his car into the garage and that you were both in the carriage house. When I found the police officer unconscious in his squad, I rang 911 and came inside looking for you."

Harry's narrative stalled at this point. His eyes glazed over. Another time, years ago, Harry had come home looking for Ric and me. He had found us embraced in a long deep kiss heavy with the promise of much more. He seemed to push the memory away and continued the story.

"I called out for you and realized you must be in the carriage house. I tried the intercom. I found you sprawled on the floor. My God Grace, your face was cherry red. You were barely breathing when I called the paramedics."

The phone on the nightstand rang and interrupted his story. Harry lifted the receiver from the cradle and identified himself. "Harry Marsden. Yes. She'll be fine. They're keeping her overnight. Have you found out anything?" Harry listened for a few moments. "I see. Thank you for the call. What? Oh, yes. I'll tell her." He hung up. "That was Officer Peterson. The police found a commercial type canister rigged with a thin needle nose hose. The hose was jammed under the side door and there were marks indicating that someone dug out enough wood in the jamb to allow the thin hose to be passed through into the carriage house. They didn't find any fingerprints. They're checking sources where these canisters could be sold and if any were recently. Oh, Officer Peterson said to tell you he's glad you're okay."

Before Harry could pick up the thread of his story, the second call came through. I picked up the phone this time. Karen was bursting to tell me about the craziness that went on in Pine Marsh the day before. I covered the mouthpiece and told him it was Karen.

He nodded his head. "Why don't you two have a chat while I go find a cup of tea?" He smiled and bent over the bed and kissed my forehead.

Seven minutes and an earful later, I had the scenario. Ric and Karen arrived just after Harry had called for help. Karen screamed when she saw me 'lifeless' on the ground. Ric unloaded a punch that dropped Harry. Karen screamed again. Harry got to his knees and then his feet while Ric was shouting oaths at him. Harry lunged at Ric knocking him off his feet and carrying them onto the lawn with his momentum. Karen screamed. They were wrestling on the ground when the sound of the sirens apparently slowed the fighting. She had heard Ric shout, "Now you'll get what you deserve you bastard."

"You bloody ass, I called them," had been Harry's answer.

I thanked Karen for the play by play, telling her Howard Cosell couldn't have done better and I promised to call her tomorrow.

When Harry returned I patted a place on the bed. I reached up and stroked his face. He winced. His grin formed lopsided as he confirmed, "he packs a mean punch!" He had guessed what Karen and I had discussed.

"My poor darling," I sympathized. "I understand from Karen that you gave as good as you got."

Harry grinned again; then his smile vanished. "Kramer still loves you. He must have suspected me all along. He didn't stop to ask what happened, just sucker punched me when I was trying to calm Karen's hysterics."

I told Harry about my earlier conversation with Ric. Waiting for the dam to burst I kept my eyes averted. No explosion came. I looked up.

"It could play that way couldn't it? I mean the last time he saw me before this 'bride' business I acted like a raving madman."

"I thought you'd be furious at his implication? I was I almost threw coffee in his face."

Harry grinned at my declaration. "I've no special place in my heart for Ric Kramer, but he's a good cop. He'd be a fool if he didn't think that way. No, he's a good cop. Except he's looking in the wrong direction about this whole thing because of his feelings for you. This is craziness. No one has a line on this that makes any sense. You're almost killed and for what, so he could investigate an empty trunk!"

"What did you say?"

"I said the man is letting his feelings cloud his..."

"No, I mean about the trunk," I interrupted. "You said it was empty, but that's not so. Harry it was filled with diaries and journals and papers."

"The bloody thing was absolutely empty, Grace."

"When did you check it? What about the other trunk?"

"Well I didn't actually check it. I just remember everything in a hodgepodge way. Later in the hospital I remembered wondering why would you spend so much time in there with an empty trunk? I must have noticed it was empty when I lifted you off the garage floor. I haven't been home since."

I realized how exhausted he looked.

"Go home darling. Get some rest." He started to protest, but I put my fingers against his lips.

"I'm tired now. Go home get a good night sleep and be back here for breakfast. In fact, bring breakfast." I placed my order for lox and bagels from Golda's Deli. I didn't think the doctors would sanction a Mimosa; I settled for fresh Papaya juice. After an especially tender kiss, the mood, or his bruised jaw, Harry left wishing me, "Pleasant dreams, darling."

I wanted him to get some rest. More than spousal concern motivated the request. I wanted him to leave. I needed to think. *An empty trunk. My attacker must have removed everything. That would have taken several trips. Where had he parked? Wouldn't that be risky—that many trips in and out of the carriage house? The fresh air, let in from all those trips was probably what saved my life. What was in those journals that was so important? Wait a minute.*

My memory was starting to sharpen and focus. I forced myself to remember. *Yes!* Excitedly, but cautiously, I tested my ability to stand up. A little wobbly but I wasn't going to topple. I worked my way to the closet, holding on to the furniture for support like an eight month old discovering from 'here to there.' I reached the closet. Inside I groped the old pants with the big pockets. God bless cargo pockets!

CHAPTER SEVENTEEN

The journal I had folded and shoved inside the roomy pocket was still there. I was too excited to be still; I did a little victory dance ala Iggie Woods in the end zone. Unlike Iggie, I got dizzy and collapsed more than sat into the chair next to the bed. I settled down to read. It seemed that this was the only surviving journal.

I knew after the first page that this journal would answer my questions. Maybe this account of years gone by had been saved so that a fifty-year-old wrong could be righted. I was certain that this journal could explain the personal tragedy in my own family.

Sister A's writing was small and her letters were well formed. The journal was easy reading. Page after page made mention of people in her daily life at the college. Then, the story of a lovely girl named Cecilia began to unfold. I could almost hear Sister's voice as I read her words about a charming Irish girl with a fairy tale romance.

May 17, 1941
We have a new attendant for our dining hall. Her name is Cecilia Doyle. She's a lovely girl and I give her every credit for making so much of herself already. Regina College's policy, to offer several scholarships to bright students from abroad, enabled her to become one of three gifted and fortunate

recipients. She came to America in 1939 with a steamer trunk filled with her past from Ireland. She had no sponsor in America, but was immediately befriended by several nuns at the College. Soon after her arrival, she sought work on campus to earn money for her expenses. She has been working in the dining room, setting, serving, and clearing for each meal. Her sweet charm and abilities were always appreciated by all of us. With graduation a month away, we know we'll be losing Eileen Maloney and Margaret Mary Canon.

I flipped forward, anxious to find more about Cecilia. I stopped at a page close to back of the journal.

December 6, 1941

Our lovely Cecilia is having her Presentation Tea later this evening. I'm helping Sister Angelicus pick and prepare a bouquet from our rose garden for the occasion. I stopped by Cecilia's room a little while ago to ask about her favorite color for the flowers. She was just slipping into her fancy dress. Oh, she looked radiant. The dress is perfect for her, a bit dreamy and old-fashioned. It suits her. She looked absolutely lovely and with the sunlight streaming in her room, lighting the pastel curtains and coverlet, she looked like a watercolor by Monet. I asked her if she would wait a moment and let me fetch my new_camera. It took me forever to get my focus. She was ever so patient. With all she had on her mind, I shouldn't wonder she didn't fidget.

My fingers felt stiff as I turned the page and reached for

the picture tucked into the journal. I stared at a photo of a lovely young girl in a beautiful beaded gown. She looked almost like a child in dress-up. The picture was faded, but even the years couldn't disguise the strong family resemblance between sisters. Looking at the photo was like looking at a younger version of my own mother. Tears filled my eyes as my brain registered that I was staring at my Aunt Cecilia.

I flipped the pages anxious to learn more. Sister A mentioned that Cecilia was marrying a young man named Tommy who had been to University and from all accounts would go far.

December 7, 1941

So much has happened already today and the day is only half gone. I have some time before I meet Sister Angelicus in the new library. The dedication was a wonderful ceremony. Monsignor said Mass and several local dignitaries were present. I was introduced to the Mayor of Chicago, Edward Kelly. Seemed like a nice man. The number people who attended the ceremony surprised me. The absence of Cecilia astonished me.

Several of the girls reported her absent from her duties as Tea Mistress. They had to get the key from Sister Phillip so they could prepare tea. Refreshments were a tiny bit late in being served. The other Sisters said that was an extremely rare occurrence. Sister went to Cecilia's room thinking she might be ill. Instead, she found a carelessly packed up room and a hasty note of explanation. Apparently, Cecilia had decided to break off her engagement and was too embarrassed to stay and face everyone. Her best friend Sheila had the unpleasant task of telling the fiancée he'd been jilted. I expected more from Cecilia, we all did. That young man looked pale and out of sorts after the news. He and his family had attended the dedication. His father's company had done some masonry work in the new library. I wish Cecilia well wherever she went off to. Back home to Ireland I suspect. Such a shame. She seemed so happy last night. Maybe the reality of the step she was about to take became clear to her. I'm taking photos this afternoon in the new library. Some of the nuns want to pose a group picture in front of the fireplace. It's a beautiful setting. The fireplace has a lovely front piece. I wish Cecilia could be there. She was always sending photos home to her aunt and sister. I will miss her.

After that entry, the diary was filled with accounts of Pearl Harbor and the effect it had on the college. Sister wrote several pages concerning the bizarre accident involving Karl Bauer that same day. She was the unfortunate person who discovered his body in the library. She probably never got a chance to take pictures that day. I wonder if the nuns ever got their group photo? It wasn't tucked in the pages. The diary went on to describe events following that Sunday including newspaper clippings of doings in the community. How typical of Sister Andrew to be so thorough. Thanks to her penchant for tying up loose ends, I finally had names to track. More importantly, I finally knew, beyond all doubt, the identity of the Rosary Bride.

CHAPTER EIGHTEEN

I climbed into bed more tired than I imagined and tucked the folded journal under my pillow. The door to my room opened and a new face came forward to minister to me.

"Hello, Mrs. Marsden. I'm LaVonda Robbins and I'll be taking care of you tonight." My night nurse smiled at me with a perfect set of pearly whites. Her cocoa toned skin was flawless around that smile except for a network of laugh lines around soft brown eyes. Her shoulder length hair was corn rolled and braided with small colorful beads incorporated into the braided lengths.

In spite of my condition, I felt a familiar twitch in my fingers as the synapses fired in my brain and I began to envision that braiding pattern. LaVonda shook her head from side to side catapulting bead against bead making a click, click, clicking sound. For a split second I glimpsed the crumbled wall of the firebox and heard the click, click, clicking of the beads released from their grave. I tensed and in that moment, LaVonda must have seen my expression. She rushed to the wrong conclusion. "C'mon Sweetie. You look like you seen a ghost. CM poisoning can be nasty stuff. Makes you uneasy and jittery. I'm here all night, Honey, right down the hall. You need anything, you press this here button." She motioned to the call button clipped close to my pillow. "That good lookin' man of yours? He'll be a few doors down spendin' the night.

You see, Honey. You got nothin' to fuss about."

LaVonda smoothed my blanket, checked the IV drip, and filled my water pitcher in preparation to leave. She turned back to the bed. "Oh, I almost forgot. That hunk of a husband of yours give me this for you." She pulled a short length of colored cloth tubing from her pocket and handed it to me. I recognized it as Harry's 'croakie,' the thin strap that holds his sunglasses on his head. I smiled at the thought of him racking his brain to get something to me. He must be wearing loafers, or I'd be holding shoelaces. The light went out noiselessly and I felt rather than saw my nurse leave the room.

In the quiet of the dark thoughts of my mother's anguish all those years, never knowing what happened to her sister swirled in my head.

As a young girl, she must have felt abandoned by the older sister she adored. I had read some of the last letters she received from Cecilia. Reading those letters reminded me that my mother used to be called Maggie rather than the Peggy everyone knew her by in this country.

She always explained that the name Peggy was more American sounding and that was why she changed it. She told me that many people gave their old-fashioned names a modern spin, especially after the war. I always thought she never wanted to be called Maggie because that had been the nickname Cecilia had given her. How would she feel now, knowing that all these years she had been living within miles of her sister's tomb? Of course, *she* already knew. Everyone else could wait. I had no one to tell until morning.

I shuddered as I thought of all the hours I had spent in the library just a few feet from that fireplace. I felt relieved that my mother had been spared the horror of this discovery.

I drifted off to sleep. A nurse came in to wake me up to

give me a sleeping pill. I remembered thinking that was only a comedy gag. She wasn't LaVonda. She approached my bed and I realized the she wasn't a nurse at all. Karen was standing over my bed. I smiled and asked what she was doing here. She didn't answer. The roomed seemed colder. I wondered if anyone had adjusted the temperature. I asked Karen to check, or to bring me a blanket. Then she wasn't Karen.

There was a young girl in my room. She wore a tattered gown that hung in shimmering strips of lace from her wasted frame. The look of anguish on her face broke my heart and I began to weep hot tears of frustration for her. Haunted eyes searched my face for recognition and I slowly shook my head from side to side, in a movement of disbelief and fear. She raised her hand, but inexplicably the flesh was gone, leaving only bony fingers, one slightly crooked as though inviting me to follow. I screamed, "No."

A baby began to cry; her look admonished me to be quiet. She lifted a bundle from the floor and held her arms in a cradle position. Her lips moved in a soundless lullaby, her body swayed slightly from side to side. The movement dislodged some beads from her gown. They fell on my bed. I picked them up one by one and felt a sense of *de ja vu*. I leaned toward her, stretching out my hand in an effort to return them. I could see what she held in her arms. Her silent ministrations were to a bloody embryo suckling at her hollow breast!

My screams stopped when the nausea began. Two nurses rushed to my room and found me vomiting and choking. I had wrapped my arms around myself in a desperate fetal position, my head buried against my chest. The touch of their hands on my hot skin felt clammy and rotting.

"She's here. She's here."

"Mrs. Marsden, who's here? We're trying to help you.

Please Mrs. Marsden, let us help you."

A sour stench filled my nostrils. I searched the room frantically for the specter.

"Can't you smell it? Oh God, it's death," I moaned.

A violent shiver shook my body. The hospital gown was soaked through with perspiration. My teeth chattered, making a clicking sound like the beads on her dress. Larger, stronger hands grasped my shoulders, pulled me up from the bed, and shook me. These hands were cool. I felt safe. Another sound reached my subconscious. The voice was firm and calm and pushed the fear out of my head.

"Harry!" My arms wrapped around him in a heartbeat. I felt strength surging from him, penetrating the thin fabric of my gown, and filling my body.

"You're all right darling," Harry soothed. "You're all right."

"She was here Harry. The Rosary Bride was here. She wanted me to follow her. Oh God, Harry, there was a baby. Only it wasn't," I stuttered.

"Hush, Gracie. It was a dream. There was no one here."

"She was here, she was. I'll prove it. Look at these." I opened my right hand, which I had kept clenched during this entire time. My fingers uncurled one at a time. Harry's expression was one of concern as he looked down at my hand. Four pinkish spots, where the sweat on my palm had diluted the blood that still oozed from the gouges my nails had dug. The underside of each nail was wet with pieces of skin and droplets of blood.

I stared down at my hand in disbelief.

"My God, Grace." His voice forced my head up to look at him.

"There were four beads from her dress. Harry, where did

they go? I was holding them. I know I was. I tried to give them back to her."

"It was a nightmare, a hellishly real nightmare. That is all, Grace. You're not quite well yet. Carbon monoxide poisoning can cause some residual hallucinations."

"Harry, it was real. She was real. I was as close to her as I am to you. It couldn't have been a dream. She was in torment." I shivered under the thin hospital gown.

"Grace, stop it. It was a terrible dream, but that is all it was. Come on old girl, don't go Shirley MacLaine on me."

I looked around the room and all did seem normal. Nothing spectral at all. "Maybe it was a dream." Wanting desperately to believe that explanation, I relaxed and leaned against Harry. He helped me out of bed and steadied me as I stood up. One nurse led me to the bathroom where she turned on the shower full force and helped me to remove my gown. She adjusted the water temperature and gently guided me behind the curtain.

The warm spray on my body brought sense back to my brain. 'How can I possibly think there is a fifty year old ghost haunting my hospital room?' The odor of fear rinsed from my body and slid away from my being like the soap suds on their journey from my shoulders to the drain. The friction from the slightly scratchy towel on my skin completed the catharsis. An experience as normal as drying off my body felt comforting. A clean gown was on the hook on the back of the door. I slipped the fabric over my head and again felt the satisfaction of normalcy.

Inside the room, the window had been opened slightly. I stopped in from of it and greedily gulped at the fresh air like a hungry guppy in a neglected aquarium. The bed had been changed. I slid between cool, smooth sheets top sheet tight against bottom. The feel of cotton against my skin was therapeutic. I wanted to stretch and sink further into its depths. I realized that the pill my nurse had given me in the bathroom had started to work. My smile assured Harry that I was feeling better My eyelids were staying closed longer between blinks. It became harder to pull them apart. I knew I had to talk fast. My sleep slowed fingers pulled the journal from under the pillow and pushed it toward him. Harry rescued it from tumbling to the floor.

"This the one." My speech slurred. "I know whereta look."

"We, darling," Harry whispered as he tucked the journal from his hip pocket. He pulled the covers up around my shoulders and gently kissed my forehead.

My hand jerked up to grab his shirt to hold him. "Doan go," I murmured.

"I'll be right here until you fall asleep."

I mumbled a sleepy, "Wuv you."

CHAPTER NINETEEN

I woke up in great spirits in spite of the lingering memory of the night before. I felt much better. My mind seemed clear and fresh like someone had opened a window in a stuffy room. I showered again, wrapped myself in my 'one size fits all' robe, and waited for Harry to arrive with breakfast. I had asked the floor nurse for a rubber band to do up my hair. She brought me the scrawniest rubber band I had ever seen. It was the only one she could find. I attempted to brush my hair back off my face and secure it at the nape of my neck. The band snapped as I wound it around my fingers. My hair jumped back across my shoulders and fell like a curtain on either side of my face.

"Damn!"

"This must be the right room," I heard in a stage whisper.

Harry entered the room pushing a rolling cart in front of him like a street vendor. The cart was set with two place settings of our china, silverware, and crystal. Breakfast was presented as elegantly as any ever served at Hugo's Market. The center of the cart held a Waterford vase filled with multicolored snaps, pink coneflowers, and deep velvety blue delphiniums. The effect was stunning. The nurse who had followed Harry to the room now moved over a little to give two more nurses a glimpse at Harry's ingenuity. They all looked wistfully at the scene. I wasn't certain if they were coveting my husband or my breakfast. The first nurse upon the scene noticed my glance and turned away, taking the others with her.

"Harry Marsden, you are incredible!" I threw my arms around his neck. He humbly submitted to my kisses.

"You ain't seen nothin' yet, Ma'am," he drawled in his best Gary Cooper.

From the bottom shelf, he produced a tote filled with a neatly folded lavender sweatshirt and pants, lavender bra and panties, a purple polo and purple socks. He had even packed my Reeboks with the purple trim.

"You must have enjoyed yourself in my drawers this morning!" The implication was broad and intended. My smile told him more.

"Gracie, now?" He laughed at my obvious tease. He stepped toward me, as though to follow my lead. Instead, he fished into his pockets and handed me my lipstick, mascara, and hair bands.

"Now I am impressed. Any man can fool with underwear!" I dressed quickly. I hadn't realized how hungry I felt. That seemed like a good sign.

I sipped my coffee and devoured a bagel, while Harry deftly manipulated my hair into a French braid. I had discovered this talent early in our relationship. It seemed he had spent many hours helping Hannah get ready when they were little. He became so good at working her hair, that when they were older and Hannah had a date, she would enlist Harry as her hairdresser. I wasn't about to let him get rusty. I was on my second bagel, slathering the bottom half with chive cream cheese and piling on the lox when Harry, having completed my coiffure, joined me.

"I've already been on the phone this morning, calling in some markers and putting a good investigator on the information in the journal. We should have the first faxes coming in this afternoon, hopefully before your homecoming bash."

I raised an eyebrow at his words.

"Well, your family insisted. I was outnumbered," he sputtered. "They just want to see for themselves that you're We'll have plenty of time to open Karl's trunk before they arrive."

"We're lucky to have this one. If we hadn't left it in Walter's Rover whoever did this would have its contents as well," I commented philosophically between bites.

"Oh yes," answered Harry sarcastically, "very lucky indeed. Grace, if finding out once and for all about your aunt weren't so important to you I'd have kicked that bloody trunk into the marsh myself," he exploded.

"I know, I know." I finished eating and carefully packed my dirty dishes.

After what seemed like an interminable wait for the doctor to release me, we pulled out of the hospital's parking lot.

"Can we drive to Mount Carmel?"

Harry knew I needed to *talk* things over with my mother. He drove me to the sprawling cemetery in Hillside and I dutifully directed him round the curving roads that separate yet connect the entire property. He knew I'd spend some time at her grave so after a few minutes spent paying his own respects, Harry drifted toward a small group of people assembled a few gravesides west of my mother's resting place. It was a tour group headed by Chicago ghost buster Richard Crowe. They were leaving the grave of the Italian Bride and heading for Al Capone's bit of turf. I noticed Harry walking with them.

It hit me as ironic that another 'bride' had been in my life for many years. As a local high school student I made the customary nocturnal pilgrimage to Peabody's Tomb and the Italian Bride's grave. Now I stood fifteen feet away, at my mother's grave, telling her that I thought I knew what happened to her sister all those years ago. Another bride with no future.

I was thinking about how desperate someone must be to come after me so boldly. What other secrets would the papers in that trunk have revealed? Harry was right about the danger. Would there be another attempt? Would the third time be the charm? For him? For me?

The gravel near the road crunched under someone's feet. My pulse quickened and I tensed, ready to run.

"Good lord, they should issue charts to help find your way. I've had a hell of a time finding my way back. Ah, pardon me." Harry glanced upwards and intoned an apology for the profanity. "Did you have a good chat with your mum?" he asked gently.

"Yes. She's keeping an eye on you for me." I laughed as I took his arm and we walked back to the car.

Some people feel creepy in a cemetery. I feel better after I've visited. After all, you know what they say. It's the live ones you have to watch out for.

As we left the cemetery, I pointed out landmarks, the small mausoleum on the right marked Rizzo and the huge pine tree with the stone bench under it. "Just turn right at both of those markers and you'll be on target. You don't need a map."

We were turning onto Wolf Road when an idea began to form. "Harry, we still have time. I want to go to Regina. I need to talk to Janet Henry."

"The alumni department coordinator? What on earth for?" Harry's voice strained as he cut off two cars to get to the right lane so he could take Harrison Street to the 290 on ramp. He was already obliging me but I knew he'd like an explanation.

"You gave me the idea darling with your talk about issuing charts. There must be hundreds of charts and blueprints of the college. If we can find the ones that date back to 1941, we can see if there were other dorm rooms and maybe track down who lived in them. There must be records of room assignments."

"That would be a long shot, darling."

"It might be the only shot we have." Was there a chance to track down proof positive after all this time? Did I want to know absolutely what I only suspected? I had more questions than answers. I needed the guts to follow through.

We pulled into the circular drive and lucked into a parking space. "Oh, sorry darling," Harry began. "I forgot to take your parking pass out of the Rover. You must have put it on the visor when Walter drove you to Regina. Can we still park here?"

"It's not in the Rover. Ric found it at Gertrude's house and returned it to me Sunday. It's here in my wallet. We're fine right here." I produced the pass and placed it in the window.

"Lucky for you I brought that purse," smirked Harry. More luck prevailed when Janet was in her office. Normally her day off, she had been called in to assist with last minute details for the gala Benefactor's Ball that Regina was hosting that night.

Chapter Twenty

"Hi, Janet, have you got a minute."

"Oh, hi, Grace. A minute is about all I have. You can't believe the number of last minute calls from people who want to attend because of the, well, you know. I'm glad you stopped by. Sister Claire asked me to mail this to you." She handed me a large manila envelope.

"Thanks, Janet. All the publicity must be making more work for you," I sympathized, trying to figure out how to add my request to her burden.

Harry handled that. Janet was beleaguered by work but soon beguiled by my husband. He had warmed up her cup of coffee, noticing I'm sure that there were opened sugar packets near the coffeepot and that the dredges were lighter than black. When he put on the 'Brit' and asked 'one lump or two?' she was hooked. Harry got her to talking about all the changes that have been made through the years. Janet at one point raised her hand in a gesture of frustration at all the archival material at Regina. It was then that Harry proposed the Herculean task of putting together a tableau of those changes. Janet agreed that alumnus would probably be interested in seeing how their floor plan compared with classes before and since and how the footprint of the college had changed.

"So Janet, if you can arrange for someone to gather up all those plans, I'll organize and record them." Harry beamed at her. "I can have them ready for reunion in June."

"Oh, that's wonderful. The students and alumni would really enjoy those descriptions. For instance, not everyone knows that this room was converted to offices in the seventies. Before that, this was the Sisters' Hall. We have albums in the back with a list of all the brides who had their Presentation Tea with the nuns in this room over the past twenty years. The fireplace has been screened off and our conference table blocks the door to the short hall and to the 'L'."

Harry and Janet walked out of the office, Janet still spewing college history. I lingered for a moment, trying to imagine those years gone by. I closed my eyes and tried to recall the vision of pictures I had seen in anniversary issues of the college's yearbook. I knew about the tradition from my aunt's diary. My mother had read the description of Aunt Cecilia's presentation tea to me many, many times. As a child, I had thought there could be nothing more romantic.

I forced my mind's eye to see now the faded words on the yellowed linen pages. I rubbed my hands together for warmth against the chill in the empty room. Harry and Janet's voices quieted as they continued down the corridor. I zipped up my jacket against the subtle changes that were happening right before my eyes. The room grew colder and the lights dimmed. I strained to see the far wall clearly, like staring into a fog waiting for an object to focus.

Suddenly my chilled brain began to recall the story that I had heard so many times as clearly as though a narrator in my head reviewed the events of all those years ago.

December 1941
The Dominican nuns, a cloistered community, were not allowed to leave the College to attend

weddings. A wonderful tradition, started years before, allowed the nuns to see the bride in her finery. Before the wedding day, a student arranged for time in the Sisters' Hall. Tea and sandwiches were served and the bride wore her gown. The bride also brought a book for the nuns to sign with their congratulations and wishes. These gatherings were usually small and, of course, sans men.

Cecilia had broken her promise of secrecy to Tommy several times. She rationalized that she would have told Tommy why they had to move up their wedding, but he had been out of town for the last three weeks. She knew he would do what was right, so she happily made all the plans herself. She asked Mrs. Marvin to prepare some sandwiches and schedule two students to help serve. Cecilia asked her best friend, Sheila Conners, to be her maid of honor and to attend the Tea.

Revealing her shock at the wedding announcement, Sheila eagerly informed Cecilia that Tommy was becoming friendly with a judge's daughter since a judge could help his career. She hurried to repeat her mother's tidbit that Tommy was visiting the judge's Palm Beach residence. Cecilia always suspected that Sheila had an enormous crush on Tommy. Recently, at the Conners' home, Elizabeth, her older sister had confirmed Sheila's obsession with Tommy. Sheila never admitted to it, but what other explanation could explain why Sheila would try to drive a wedge between Cecilia and Tommy. Cecilia believed what Tommy had told her, that he was at Officer Training School and that couldn't call her during training. Cecilia happily awaited his arrival on the sixth at their regular time.

In spite of Sheila's jealousy, or maybe because of it, Sheila agreed to be her maid of honor. Cecilia hoped that eventually her friend would share in her happiness.

All that behind her, Cecilia stood in her room on the night of the sixth preparing for her Tea. She carefully groomed her long, silky hair and pulled it back from her face. She secured her strawberry blonde tresses at the nape of her neck with a mother of pearl clip. As she stepped into a creamy white gown covered with hundreds of bugle beads in the palest shades of aqua, violet, and pink, she is startled to find herself wearing her mother's gown so soon. The special legacy is part of the past Cecilia brought with her to America two years before. After the wedding, she will pack it up and send it off to Maggie for her to wear someday.

She smiled recalling thoughts of her mother and knows she would have shared her joy as she prepares for the most wonderful day of her life. Her mother would have guided her through the frightening and joyful times over the next important months. Thinking of her father, she realized her new responsibility overshadowed any regrets he might have voiced over her lost opportunity in America.

Concerning the wedding banns, Cecilia planned to talk to Father Brenner the next day after mass. She will ask the priest to perform the ceremony in the chapel as soon as possible, after the wedding banns are published. Many things in her life at Regina will change because of her wedding. Tomorrow will be her last day as Tea Mistress. The dedication of the new library would be preceded by a special mass and followed by a Tea.

She jumped at a knock at the door. Slowly admitting her friend, she hoped Sheila won't want to visit too much after the tea. The tea begins at 5:00 and ends at 6:30. Cecilia wanted to rest a little before Tommy came through the tunnels. She really needed her rest lately. She wanted to be rested and radiant when she told him her wonderful news.

She stood aside as Sheila rushed into the room, wearing a tea length, aqua gown, the bodice a solid turquoise, and the skirt a field of tiny yellow pink and violet flowers. The aqua set off Sheila's dark blonde hair and lightly tanned skin. She chided her about being late for the Sisters. Cecilia took one last look in the mirror above the dresser and put away the letter she'd been writing to her aunt. Her attempts to explain the news lie crumpled in her wastebasket; it all sounded so negative on paper. She will finish her letter tomorrow and post it Monday.

Cecilia enjoyed her presentation tea. No evening had ever been so special. She felt like a princess and wished her evening would last until midnight. Mrs. Marvin says she has never seen so many Sisters in attendance. She scurried back to the kitchen more than once to prepare more cucumber sandwiches and deviled eggs. The Sisters are wonderful to her. Sister Phillip approached her first saying, "We will all miss you and your stories." "And we shall miss your serving," chimes in Sister Anna (who always appreciates the extra potatoes Cecilia served her). "God bless you, Cecilia," comes from Sister Colletta who presented Cecilia with a beautiful ivory rosary for her to use during her wedding Mass. The gift is from all her friends. Cecilia is touched by their thoughtfulness. Even the newest nun, Sister Andrew attends, and when they sing 'Ave Maria,' her voice sounds the sweetest.

Nuns by their nature do not ask many personal questions or pry into personal issues. Cecilia confided her situation to only two Sisters. Their comments are sincere offers of best wishes for her and her fiancée. Cecilia is overwhelmed, surrounded as she is by friends, enjoying her happiness. She counts herself blessed to have found a 'second family' at Regina. Several Sisters comment on how she beams with happiness. Sister Andrew offers to take a photograph to commemorate the occasion. She has a new camera and she takes any opportunity to snap photos. Everyone giggles as they pose for the snapshot. Rotund Sister Claire hugs Cecilia impulsively. "I will pray for you, my dear." "Thank you, Sister. You will all be in my prayers too." Promptly at six-thirty, Cecilia thanked all the Sisters for attending her Presentation Tea. Following tradition, Cecilia wrapped almond candies in small squares of sheer netting and tied the tasty bundle with thin colorful ribbons. She deftly braided the ribbons in an intricate pattern she had learned from her mother. Now, she hugs each nun as she hands each a tea favor. Sheila doesn't stay to assist Cecilia with passing out the favors or making sure each nun signed the book. Cecilia is happy to do this alone. She understands that her best friend is still adjusting to the idea of Tommy marrying someone else

Cecilia returned to her room, taking twenty precious minutes to write in her diary, recording her Tea. Then she lay down for a short nap. 'The evening was so lovely. My life is so perfect, she wrote.' Cecilia wraps herself in those thoughts and closes her eyes.

The floor pitched like the deck of a small boat in choppy water. Howling winds muffled my cries for help. The night was star less, inky dark and unfriendly. I was overboard in Lake Michigan, bobbing in 50-degree water, being tossed further from the 26-foot catch that meant safety. Bone-chilling cold paralyzed my legs. Each time I pushed up from beneath a breaking wave, I sputtered and tried to fill my lungs with enough air to survive for other wave. I could expend the precious oxygen on screaming or on battling the waves. Either way, I was losing.

"Grace, Grace! Are you all right? What is it?" Harry pulled me from the water, to safety. The deck stopped pitching wildly. It swayed like a meadow of sea grass in a gentle breeze. "Darling, talk to me," Harry's voice flooded me with warmth. I opened my eyes and reality hit right between them. I was lying on the floor of the Alumni Office, twenty feet from where I had been standing two minutes ago. A thread worn Persian rug lay between the cold marble floor and me. The conference table was inches away from me.

"Harry I don't know what happened. I was standing in the middle of the room and then there was this kind of fog and terrible cold."

"Do you want me to call a doctor?" asked a worried looking Janet.

"No, of course not," I answered quickly. "I'm fine. I think I just. I don't know," I fumbled, "but I'm okay. Really, Janet, I'm fine," I assured her.

Janet walked out with us. She seemed convinced that I was fine and waved from the steps as we pulled away from the circular drive.

Harry was another story.

"Grace I think I should take you back to hospital and have them examine you."

"Harry, I'm fine. Really, I must have just overdone it."

"All right, but we're going straight home, which is where we should have gone in the first place. And, I'm calling off the Morellis until tomorrow."

I was more shaken by those few minutes then I let on. The feeling that my aunt was trying to reach me kept getting stronger. I realized I hadn't hallucinated the specter from the night before. That same bone-chilling cold was what I had felt last night, today and that day in the 'L.' In the Alumni Office, I was just yards away from that spot. I felt she wanted me to know the truth. I wasn't about to tell my 'two feet on the ground' husband *that* theory.

CHAPTER TWENTY-ONE

During the ride home, I dialed Karen's number. A male voice promptly answered the phone. His voice was very distinctive; the timber low and almost musical. It was Karen's uncle. He had retired from public life years before I had met him. Karen told me that he had been quite an orator; his speeches filled with eloquence and passion. Karen had probably forwarded her calls again. After I identified myself, Uncle Richard asked how I was feeling.

"People are so violent and cruel. We all look so normal, but who are we really? You'd best take care, my dear." He sounded so tired and sad. He had looked that way at Karen's house. I hadn't talked to him in years, but it seemed as though he had become very fatalistic in his approach to life. I supposed older people viewed their lives differently. He must be at least in his seventies. Maybe reaching that age gave you a reason to look on the grim side. Karen mentioned that her uncle had become more withdrawn and difficult in the past few years. I didn't see my dad behaving that way, but he had shared most of his life with my mother, his soul mate.

Part of the reason was probably his wife. Karen adored her aunt. She was the last person to admit to that woman's faults. Her aunt had been supportive of Karen and Ric since their mother died. Karen had been a freshman at Regina when Beth Kramer had drowned.

There had been a long investigation first by the police and then by the insurance company. The investigator had been Derek Rhodes who was later recruited by the firm Harry had worked for. Rhodes had interviewed everyone connected with the incident and seemed to be dissatisfied with the police findings. Karen and Ric were scrutinized, since they were the heirs, and that was a horrible time for both of them. Aunt Shelly flew into a rage at Rhodes' innuendoes and just about got him fired. His investigation was finally completed and the death termed accidental.

Karen's aunt had stepped into the role of surrogate mother. She never had children of her own; she wouldn't have had the time! Aunt Shelly was always on the go: chairing committees, competing in charity golf tournaments, even playing tennis at their club several times a week.

Karen had always thought them an odd couple. Her uncle recoiled from his success and power as though he would prefer obscurity. Her aunt, on the other hand, raced through each day filling it with as many people and places as twenty-four hours could decently hold. Each a slave to their own demons and delights.

"Hello, hello?" Karen's voice interrupted my thoughts like a hand waving in front of my eyes.

"Oh, sorry Karen. I guess I was a million miles away."

"How are you feeling? Are you home?"

"Harry and I are on our way now. We're opening the other trunk this afternoon. Karen, I know who the bride is. Maybe this trunk will help us find out why she died."

I heard a soft sigh and quiet click and suddenly the hairs on the back of my neck tingled. The eerie silence spread a cold dread through the hand set. I switched the phone to my other hand and wiped my palm against the fabric of my sweatshirt.

"Karen, are you there?"

My voice alerted Harry. He looked at me, querying me with an arched eyebrow. I shrugged off the feeling as Karen answered. "I thought you had call waiting and put me on hold."

"No," I answered hesitantly. "It sounded like a receiver being hung up."

"Maybe Uncle Richard stayed on to make sure I'd picked up."

"Where are you? I mean in the house, where are you?"

"I'm in the guest room. Why are you asking all these questions?" Karen sounded annoyed.

"No reason. Do you want us to wait for you?"

"You bet I do. See you there."

Harry asked if Nancy Drew and her chum were close to solving the mystery. Then his tone grew serious.

"There's no reason to think that someone won't try to kill you again Grace. I've checked with my people. It's no one they can connect to me. I'm beginning to believe Kramer's idea that this is all connected with that skeleton. Because of that and because I love you, we're turning the trunk over to the police this afternoon. Kramer will be there when we get home."

"Harry no! If the police take the trunk, they'll just bury it somewhere in storage. They don't care who she was. They don't care that some bastard killed my aunt and buried her in a wall. Maybe she was alive when," my voice ran down to a whisper.

"Gracie, don't think about that."

"What do you want me to think? No one cares. I want to find out for sure. I want to finally lay her and her baby to rest in a proper grave. The police don't care about a fifty year old homicide."

"People do care, Grace. I care more about keeping you alive than honoring the dead. You've been in danger since those trunks came into your possession. I promise you that I'll do all that I can to find out the truth. You believe that, don't you Grace?"

Harry kept his eyes glued to the road ahead. We were crossing the bridge over The Marsh. Harry maneuvered to the right and we passed the Rowe and Atwater properties. Our house is at the farthest point back from the entrance before you hit marsh and eventually the lake.

"All right," I consented as we got out of the car. "We'll give the trunk to Ric, but let's look through it first. Please Harry?" My pleading eyes, deep purple, lit with sparks from an Irish ancestor, seemingly convinced him.

"Don't suppose a quick look would compromise anything. Why not?"

My ear to ear grin answered his rhetorical question.

"All right then, let's have a go at it."

"Oh wait. I promised Karen she could be here when we opened it."

"And I told Kramer he could have it when he arrived. Which is it to be?"

"Let's open it. Karen will understand."

Harry attempted to open the lock with several keys he had purchased from two locksmiths who specialized in old luggage. None of the keys worked. In the end it was Harry's skill with the tiny files he produced from an old leather case that opened the stubborn mechanism. He didn't explain why he knew how to pick a lock. I suppose fingers nimble enough to plait hair might find other uses as well.

The click of the metal tumbler falling into place was loud

in the small area of the garage. I realized that I had been holding my breath and braiding a piece of twine that had been used to move the trunk to the garage. Harry slowly raised the lid. The contents appeared normal enough. My thoughts jumped back to what Uncle Richard had said this afternoon about everyone seeming normal, but who really knows what we are. The sound of that sorrowful sigh replayed in my head.

"Darling, you're shivering. Are you all right?" Harry's face was lined with concern.

"Yes, I'm fine. I guess I thought there would be more."

The trunk contained mostly clothes, some books, and a few pictures. I lifted out the books and paged through them. They were in German. Harry was going through the clothes. I had just picked up two smaller books when a low whistle riveted my attention.

Harry stretched out his hand, turned it palm up, and slowly opened his fingers.

"That's evidence you're withholding."

Ric's voice startled me. I bumped Harry's hand. He quickly clenched his fist saving four tiny beads from falling to the floor.

"Ric, you startled me," I stammered.

"Is this your idea of turning over evidence, Marsden?" The barb was unmistakable.

"It's my fault Ric, I wanted to take a peek before we turned it over."

"Still doing the explaining, eh, Gracie?"

"What's that supposed to mean, Kramer?" Harry stood up and walked toward Ric.

"Ask your wife."

"I'm asking you."

"Will you two stop it? We're on the verge of solving a

fifty-year-old crime and you're playing games. Look at these."
I pried open Harry's fingers, much like a child searching a
parent's hand for goodies. The tiny beads shimmered aqua,
pink, and violet.

"Harry found these in Karl's uniform. He must be the
murderer. I found these same beads on the floor in the library.
After he sealed her up in the cavity, he must have found some
stray beads on the floor and put them in his pocket."

"But he died before he could get rid of the evidence."
added Harry.

Ric and I both stared at Harry.

"How can you possibly know that?"

"Because there is a brownish stain on this shirt that I'll bet
is fifty year old blood."

I picked up the thread. "So, before he could throw out the
beads, he died and the undertaker just tossed his effects into a
bag that ended up in his trunk. That's it. Harry that's brilliant."
I gushed a little more than normal for Ric's benefit.

"What's brilliant?" Karen asked from the doorway.

"We solved the mystery of the Rosary Bride. Karl Bauer
the handyman, killed her and placed her body in the fireplace
wall." But before he could—"

"Who killed Bauer?" Ric's quiet question stopped me
cold. "You see, we police can conduct a successful
investigation in spite of civilian interference. I had some men
check the old files in the basement for the report on Bauer's
death. You have to keep in mind that December seventh was a
crazy day and one accidental death fell short of being important
on the day this country charged into war."

"Ric, you're not on one of your lecture tours," Karen
complained.

"Bottom line is, since the department knew people would
be enlisting left and right, the Chief decided to train a new

Medical Examiner a.s.a.p. Even though Bauer was tagged an accident, since he had no family, they figured it would be okay to practice on him."

"If they knew from the autopsy that it was a homicide why didn't they change the cause of death?" Harry asked.

"They didn't know because the raw recruit who recorded the findings didn't know what he had. Anyway, the report was filed the body buried, and the man forgotten. When the sergeant found the report we showed it to our ME, Dr. Lathrop. He believes that the fatal blow was the crushing one to the top of the skull. But what no one picked up on was that there was another blow to the front of the face, that was sufficient to stun a person but not kill."

"So you're saying that someone hit him in the face, knocked him into the bookcase and that's how the statue landed on his head?" That was Karen's condensed version.

"No, I had forensics check angles and the statue couldn't have just fallen. The angle supports the theory that he was struck in such a way that the point of origination of descent was frontal."

"The Inspector is telling us that Karl Bauer was struck by someone standing in front of him."

"You don't seem too surprised by all of this Marsden."

"I'm not. I've been looking at the pattern of stains on his shirt and your scenario makes sense." Harry handed Ric the uniform shirt, the name Karl on the pocket, almost obliterated by the brown stain. "How tall do your boys think the killer was?"

"Again, working from the angle, about 6'2" give or take a skosh," came Ric's reply. He looked at me across the trunk.

"Since we seem to be back to square one, except now we have two murders, let's at least get comfortable. And maybe get some coffee?"

Chapter Twenty–Two

I ushered everyone into the great room and walked into the kitchen to make coffee. Strands of hair had escaped Harry's handiwork. I reached into my pocket for one of the hair combs Harry had brought me this morning. My fingers touched the small book from the trunk. I must have slipped it into my pocket when Ric arrived. In a past life, I must have been a kleptomaniac.

Unruly hair forgotten, coffee maker standing idle, I began to thumb through the book. Expecting German, I was pleased to see English.

The book appeared to be a journal or diary of sorts. The early pages mentioned projects the nuns requested. Entries about doings at the school, tools purchased for his woodcarving, a new station wagon for the nuns. The entries reflected contentment laced with certain loneliness.

Then, a brief mention of the new Tea Mistress. My mind picked up the pace now. More entries pertaining to Miss Cecilia. *Yes, my God. He did know her.* The words were plain and the meaning was becoming clearer with every entry. My eyes were racing down the page looking for names, anything to connect my aunt to someone that could have killed her.

Karl Bauer had fallen in love with this young college lady with whom he had barely spoken throughout an entire school year!

'Maybe he did kill her. Ric's evidence could be wrong. Perhaps he snapped when she fell in love with the Tommy in Sister A's account. It could have been a fatal attraction kind of thing.' I reached the end of the diary, no closer to really knowing anything.

"Are you grinding the beans one by one?" Karen really could be a pain in the ass sometimes.

"Should be just about ready."

"Not if you don't plug in these modern conveniences I shower you with." Harry grinned and pushed the plug into the outlet. The electrical arch that followed jolted and slammed Harry into the table ten feet across the room. The wall sparked blue light. Karen screamed when the lights went out. The smell of burning flesh reached my nostrils just as Karen hit another high note.

Ric remembered the layout of the house. While he moved through the dark, I carefully crawled to where I had seen Harry fall the instant before darkness.

"Harry, Harry!" I touched his shoulder in the dark. He was so still. "Harry," panic rising in my voice. Just then, the lights came on. Harry was unconscious. His right hand was badly burned around the fingertips. His color terrified me.

"He's not breathing! Karen, call an ambulance." Ric rushed past his sister as she reached for the phone. He knelt next to Harry, putting his fingers on his neck for a pulse.

"No pulse, help me get him on his back!" Ric immediately started CPR. I knelt there terrified; hot tears streaming down my face.

"Will he be all right?" I asked between choking sobs. Ric kept up his rhythm, but his eyes searched mine for something.

I felt Karen's arms around my shoulders and then I heard the thin wail of a siren. The sound grew until the wail was inhuman; like a howl from the darkness. I felt that *she* was in the room again. Karen touched me and I pulled away from her. *God, am I losing my mind?* Karen took my hand again and pulled me toward the door.

The paramedics took over from Ric. They got a pulse, it was getting stronger. They started an IV and dressed the burn on Harry's hand before they placed him on the litter.

I followed the gurney out to the ambulance. Ric was handling the sheriff's police who had arrived within minutes of the ambulance. Karen was talking to one of the paramedics.

"Lucky for you ladies that neither one of you plugged in that pot. That jolt would have killed you for sure."

I caught the look that passed between Ric and Karen. Ric glanced at me, realized that I caught the exchange, and looked away. The paramedic touched my arm.

"Ma'am. He's still unconscious but stable enough to move. You can ride back here."

He helped me into the ambulance. I picked up Harry's left hand. It was warm. Alive. I wiped tears from my face when Harry began to stir. His eyelids fluttered and then opened. He seemed disoriented, his eyes vacant. I smiled brightly and struggled to keep my voice steady.

"Thank God you're alive. I love you, I'm—" I choked back my last words trying to apologize for having put him in jeopardy. Harry closed his eyes, but a slight squeeze of my hand told me that he heard.

At the hospital, Harry was examined and admitted. They hooked up another IV, antibiotics for possible infection they told me. He was asleep. I wanted to spend the night at the hospital but I needed to go home and get some things. The doctor assured me that Harry would sleep through the night and that I should get all the rest I could. Karen tried to convince me to listen to the doctor's advice. In the end, the same ER nurse who had cared for me changed my mind.

She recognized me when she entered the room. She looked at Harry's chart and then back at me.

"Honey, you and this gorgeous man need to sell that house. Too many accidents. I worked ER at County and never saw a house with so many dangerous flaws. You'd be safer in the projects, child." She had delivered those comments with a grin and wink. I smiled back in appreciation of her efforts to make me feel better. She put her hand on my shoulder.

"I took good care of you last night. I'll do the same for your man. You know I will. Now go on home and rest. You look worn to a frazzle. You need to get your strength up; you're still recovering from your troubles. Now you kiss that fine man goodnight and get on home. It's his hand is hurt, honey."

I laughed at her implication. "Yes ma'am." I answered and gave her a small hug. I leaned over Harry's sleeping form, listening to his regular breathing. I tucked him in with a soft kiss and a quick prayer and asked Karen for a ride home.

"Grace, you shouldn't stay by yourself. In fact I'm surprised Ric hasn't suggested that already."

"He told me at the hospital that he was assigning a police woman to stay with me."

"That's not good enough. You've been through too much. I'll drive you home to pick up some things and then I'll take you back with me. Ric can assign a person to my house."

I was in no mood to argue. We pulled up in front of my house. Ric's car was still there. He was struggling to load the trunk into his car. Karen bounced out and hoisted an end of the trunk almost effortlessly. I marveled at how strong she was.

All the tennis and racquetball she played with her aunt at their club had kept her in marvelous shape. I wished for some of that stamina now. I felt exhausted.

I reached the back of Ric's car as he was getting ready to leave. He seemed anxious to go. I wanted to thank him for saving Harry's life. Maybe he knew.

He mumbled, "Karen filled me in on tonight. I'll have someone at her house."

Ric said he was running late for a function at Regina College honoring his aunt and three other people for their contributions of *time, treasure, and talent* to the community during the past year.

"Uncle Richard isn't feeling well, so I agreed to escort my aunt to the dinner."

"It sounds like a lovely evening. Congratulate your aunt for me." Ric's reaction was unexpected.

"Yes, I will, for a job well done. I wonder who she slept with to get this recognition." Ric's voice filled with anger.

"Ric, dammit! How dare you say that," Karen yelled.

"Come on Karen. You're the only one who doesn't see what *dear* Aunt Shelly is, a society whore! Why do you think Uncle Richard is so sick? She's taken a strong, proud man and broken his spirit with one dirty affair after another. It's only his name and money that keeps her in such demand."

"You would side with Uncle Richard. Never mind, the way he's treated her all these years. No affection, no children. I'm just surprised she never left him!" Karen shouted back furiously.

"Never left him; what a joke. She'd never want to stop being Mrs. Richard Walsh. He's given her everything that money and power could buy." Ric answered.

I knew better than to get involved in a family squabble,

and this was a doozey, but my natural curiosity got the better of me.

"If you feel this strongly about her Ric, why are you escorting her?"

Ric turned abruptly from his sister to face me.

"So she can't gloat while she sashays around with him on her arm," he explained in a softer voice. He took that opportunity to leave without a good bye or backward glance.

"Whew, you two were really hot."

"He's such an ass. Even though he's older, sometimes he thinks life is simple with easy rules to follow. Grace, my aunt is a wonderful woman. My uncle is the strange one. My mother couldn't stand the sight of him. She even tried to stop my aunt from marrying him. We never really saw much of them when mother was alive. Except for right before she died. She and Uncle Richard must have started to make some attempt at a truce of sorts. She had lunch with him at the marina. I think even took him out on The Bride."

"On the what?" I interrupted feeling a chill touch my spine when I thought of my earlier experience.

"Oh, God. I'd forgotten. I guess blocked it out, is more like it. The name of my mother's boat was The Rosary Bride. She named it that because she and my dad were married in the chapel at Regina and the boat was a wedding present from my dad. After my dad died, mother spent most of her free time on the boat, usually up at the cottage at St. Joseph. She said being on the boat reminded her of dad. I never enjoyed sailing as much as she did. Ric always sailed with her except when he was in Nam. Then I did. Except when—"

Karen's voice stopped abruptly. We both sat quietly. I watched the expression on her face, as she seemed to struggle with a familiar demon. She shook her head and smiled at me.

"Anyway, that's why I was surprised that she would take my uncle out on *The Bride*. I never really knew my aunt well until after mother was gone. I've never known Uncle Richard any other way."

It seemed important to Karen that I agreed with her reasoning.

I murmured appropriate noises while I packed a few items. Before I left, I checked Harry's office for faxes. There were several. I gathered up the faxes and my envelope from Sister Claire and stuffed them, along with the journal Harry had left on his desk, into my overnight bag.

CHAPTER TWENTY-THREE

I was silent for most of the ride to Oak Park. Karen was making small talk. Suddenly something occurred to me. "Karen, if this dinner tonight is to honor your aunt, why aren't you going?"

"I was going to go, but I thought it was more important that I be with you."

"Oh, I'm sorry. Look Karen, I really appreciate your concern and wanting to help me. You are truly a best friend, but you should be with your aunt tonight. Take me home and I'll call one of my brothers to come stay with me tonight."

"Well it's a thought, but it doesn't really matter now. By the time I take you home and get back I won't be able to get ready in time. It's no big deal. My aunt is always on some committee whose members are being honored. I'll catch the next one."

Her voice was light, but I heard the slight strain. As we exited 290 Karen turned to me. "Grace, I could make it in time if I go to my aunt's house. I have extra clothes there. I could shower, change, and be there on time. You could wait there for me. I'd just want to see the award part. I could duck out, pick you up and we could go to my place for the night. What do you think?"

I really wanted to climb into a soft bed and try to forget this entire day. I also really wanted to read everything in my tote bag, but I didn't want to disappoint Karen. "Yeah, I guess that will work. Do you think your uncle will mind?"

"No, not at all. He'll welcome the company. He likes you Grace." With that pronouncement, we pulled up to the curb in front of the Walsh home. As I opened the car door, I slipped the strap of my tote over my shoulder.

Karen settled me in the library. The room was beautifully furnished with expensive antiques and art, but there was no warmth in this room. It looked unused and even less appreciated. A Louis XIIII writing desk looked like the real McCoy, but doubted that anyone had ever sat there and penned a letter to a friend. I was certain that a quick look about would show me several first day folios, priceless books, with which to decorate a flawless room, almost flawless room. The fireplace had been used lately. Ashes still filled the box almost to the bottom of the grate. Unburned fragments hung from the metal, surrounded, and held up by the pile of ash. The mess seemed out of place in this room. My eye was drawn to a bit of bright blue in the ashes. It appeared to be fabric. "Odd, why would someone burn material?" I asked aloud. The sound of my voice broke the reverie I'd fallen into staring into the fireplace. I dismissed my criticism of Aunt Shelley's housekeeping and decided to have a look at the faxes in my tote.

I switched on a reading lamp and pulled out the sheets. There were four: one each for Cecilia Doyle, her best friend Sheila Conners, my aunt's fiancé Tommy, and the college custodian Karl Bauer. I read the brief bio on the bride. All lies! Last reported leaving Regina College to avoid marriage, the report quoted a school friend. Her family knew she'd never have left her fiancée. Karl's bio was almost as brief. It listed his birthplace, marriage, and immigration to America. The fax also included a passport photo and description. He had been very good-looking. Blond, muscular, tall. Something was tugging at my mind, but then, I heard a familiar voice.

"Mrs. Marsden. How nice to see you again."

I looked up as Richard Walsh entered the library. Actually, he stopped just inside the threshold. The man responsible for Harry's rescue extended his hand to me.

I stood up quickly to cover the distance between us. One of the faxes slipped from my lap and slid to the carpet. Uncle Richard looked at the paper, but it was his wife who stooped to retrieve it even before her nephew could. Aunt Shelly and Ric had entered the room noiselessly from another door. Ric was impeccably dressed in a black tuxedo with a deep burgundy colored cummerbund and bow tie to match. His dark good looks were set off by the crisp white shirt, the ruffled front adding a note of romance. He looked gorgeous. He knew it.

Shelly looked incredible herself. Years of sports and spas had dealt kindly with her. She could boast of well-toned, lightly muscled body that any middle-aged matron would die for. She was wearing a feminine version of a tuxedo, black satin pants with a matching jacket. Instead of a cummerbund and shirt, Shelly finished her outfit with a crisp white modified bustier. The effect was quite stunning. She moved quickly now to return the page to me with one hand, while shaking hands with the other. Her step was nimble and her handshake firm.

"Grace, it is good to see you again. We barely spoke the other night. How long has it been?" She glanced at Ric, knowing full well the last time was seven years ago when he and I were planning a week together at their Palm Springs home.

Ric's face clouded over with memories. *She really is a bitch,* I thought as I smiled at her and answered.

"I'm not sure, but that means too long." She seemed disappointed that I didn't take the bait. Ric had stood quietly through this whole exchange. His uncle had lowered himself onto the chair closest to the door. He too was quiet.

Karen came in carrying a tray for her uncle. "Maryann said you wanted dinner on a tray. She was just leaving to catch her bus. I told her I'd bring it to you."

He stood up quickly. "Bring that tray back to the kitchen. I am not in the habit of eating in the library," he finished harshly. Karen looked at her aunt for an explanation of his outburst.

"Karen dear, don't mind your uncle. He has firm ideas about what's proper and what's not. Anyway, he never comes into the library. Says he hates the quiet. I love to curl up with a Dean Koontz book in front of a picture perfect fire. I had quite a blaze going in there today. I am surprised to find him in here. I suppose he wanted a word with you Grace."

Her smile curved her mouth, but her marble-hard eyes slashed at me, like a scythe through tall grass. *She's jealous of me talking to her husband,* was my first thought. *That's too crazy!*

Ric, who had been strangely quiet, stepped into the conversation.

"You are the honoree and as your escort I cannot allow you to be late." With those out-of-character words, he settled a wrap around her shoulders and held out his left arm for her to take. His charm obviously pleased her. She smiled graciously and took his arm. They moved forward through the double doors. Ric stopped at the threshold. He half turned. "Goodnight, Grace."

He placed two fingers to his lips then turned them palm out to me in a gesture of good bye. Aunt Shelly disengaged her arm and turned to face me.

"Good-bye my dear. I don't think I shall be seeing you again...very soon," she added as an afterthought.

Both good-byes seemed so final; one rather poignant, the other almost nasty. I shivered and wished I hadn't agreed to wait for Karen. I realized that I was trapped here for at least two hours before Karen could get back and she hadn't even left. She was upstairs dressing. I fervently hoped her uncle stayed put wherever he had retreated to. Maybe he would since he didn't like this room. I resolved not to leave the library for any reason. My tote bag was brimming with reading material. I pulled another of Karl's diaries from my sack and began skimming pages for familiar names. I stopped at an entry dated fifty years ago.

December 7, 1941

I was up earlier than usual this morning. In addition to my normal duties today I had to supervise the finishing touches on the new library. The workmen the college hired arrived on time for a change. They were the same two that have been here all week. Big loafers. They're goldbricking a job that should have been done in half the time. I was worried that they'd waste time and not have the library ready at ten o'clock for the dedication. The mass was already started when I got to the library from the main entrance. I was delayed by some of the sisters who needed to find the extra key to the cupboard with the tea services. When I entered the library, I expected to see the men still on their hands and knees near the fireplace. They were off to the side sipping coffee from thermoses. I walked toward them ready to give them a dressing down for their laziness. I glanced at the fireplace and stopped in my tracks. They were finished. On closer inspection of their work, I could see that the bottom rows were a little sloppy. I was about to mention this fact when I heard the final benediction from the chapel. That meant that the guests would soon be out in the library. So I signed off on their cards and dismissed them. The double doors at the back of the Chapel opened and many of Oak Park's finest families streamed out of Mass. I spotted the Walsh family coming into the library. I'd heard stories about most of the local families from the students and the nuns. Everyone talked in front of the handyman. Mr. Walsh seemed a decent sort, his older son a carbon copy of the old man. He was learning the trade to take over the reins of the company just like his father had from his own dad. Maybe it was an uncle. They're a large family, with cousins galore. I've seen many a Walsh name at the college these past years. The youngest son, Tommy was a different sort. He took after his mother. That's what Mrs. Marvin told me. Mrs. Walsh had passed away years ago. On her deathbed, she asked that Tommy be given the opportunity to use his brains and not his hands. Well, the old man tried his best. According to Mrs. Langdon in the laundry, Tommy was wild and never appreciated the sacrifices his father and brother made to give him his chance. I know he's no good from personal experience. He never walks Miss Cecilia up to the gate and waits with her. He just leaves her standing alone in the dark. I saw him strutting across the lawn from the grotto last night. He was carrying that valise that Miss Cecilia uses when she leaves the college for the night. I left before she came out. I couldn't stand to see her go with him. She is so sweet and lovely. I almost choked with anger once when she asked me to repair the handle on that valise. I knew her secret and it tortured me to think of the liberties that 'rich boy' took with her and the lies he must have told her. It was all I could do to be civil to Tommy this morning. When Mr. Walsh asked me about the workers, I told him that I had dismissed them. I didn't tell him what I thought of his men or his son.

Tommy was quiet and distant and he missed a question his father asked him about law being better than bricklaying. Tommy looked uncomfortable when he answered his father. He mumbled an excuse and walked away. I asked Mr. Walsh why Tommy learned the trade since he was going to be a lawyer. He told me that until his mother died Tommy worked his school holidays right along with Mr. Walsh and Kevin. Just then, Kevin had noticed a rag left near the fireplace. Mr. Walsh was embarrassed by the carelessness of his men. I told him not to worry and no one would be the wiser. I crossed the tile and stooped to pick it up. I noticed something on the floor near the firebox. They were tiny beads of some sort. I can't imagine how they got there; hardly looked like anything those workmen would lose.

After that the speeches began and I tried to melt into the back of the crowd of guests in case my eyes glazed over during the speeches. I still had those beads in my hand. Why would four beads be on that floor? No one had been in the library during Mass except the workers. That's when I overheard a conversation between the girls serving at the refreshments table and learned that dear, sweet, Cecilia was missing. The girls seemed upset.

I dare say she could have at least let someone know. Mrs. Marvin was really put out especially since she had fixed up such nice sandwiches for her Tea.'

'Well, Cecilia has never missed before. I'm sure that she has a very good reason.'

'Her best friend, Sheila Conners, went up to her room with Sister Phillip. There wasn't anything there. Everything was gone.'

That was all I heard. I turned to verify this gossip, but just then the speech ended and the guests began to converge on the refreshment table I couldn't talk to them now. I saw Sister Phillip. No good! She was buttonholing some generous patrons to offer thanks and solicit more donations for the college. Then I spotted Sheila. She was talking to Tommy. It was sickening the way she threw herself at him, even here on this occasion. Some best friend. She was leaving Tommy's side, her sister Elizabeth had motioned for her to join her. As Sheila turned to Tommy to excuse herself, Elizabeth directed one millisecond look of undisguised hatred toward Tommy. I was amazed at the raw cruelty in the look. Wonder what he'd done to deserve that?

I was very polite when I approached Sheila. 'Excuse me, Miss Conners. May I have a word with you? I don't want you to think that I'm being nosy, but I overheard the tea ladies say that Cecilia, er, Miss Doyle, is gone. They said you went up with Sister Phillip and all her belongings are gone. Is that true?' Her answer was quick in coming. 'I'm not supposed to tell, but you're part of the college. I'm sure Sister Phillip didn't mean you. Cecilia is gone. She took everything. I'm shocked. After all, I'm her best friend and she didn't tell me anything. I mean, we're very close. She asked me to be her maid of honor, didn't she? There was a crumpled note in her basket telling her aunt that she was breaking off her engagement with Tommy,' she continued. 'I can't believe she would be so cruel and just run off rather than face him, and us. She'll probably go back home.'

I didn't believe for one minute that she was upset. She's one of those theater majors and it seemed to me she was playing the part of a concerned friend. 'I think it very strange that she didn't take her trunk. It's loaded up in storage,' I said to her.

'Oh, well, obviously she was in a hurry. She'll probably send for it,' she said. 'Excuse me, Karl, but I want to catch Tommy. He was so upset when I told him. I felt it was my place to tell him, I mean their meeting at my home and all. I mean, I feel responsible.'

'Just a minute. I heard that Miss Doyle had her presentation to the Sisters yesterday evening. Was she dressed in her wedding gown?'

'Of course,' Sheila said impatiently. 'That's the purpose of presentation.' Her eyes searched the room to catch a glimpse of Tommy while she answered me.

'Of course it is," I murmured. 'Did her dress have anything like this on it?' I held out my hand, palm up and uncurled my fingers. The four iridescent beads shimmered in my work-worn hand like petals off a rose fallen on hard ground. Sheila's attention returned to me. She looked at the beads. 'Yes, they were, they..." she stopped abruptly.

'Where did you get those?' her eyes locked on mine. I never noticed how green and cold her eyes were. 'Let's just say I found them in a very odd place,' I said. I dropped the beads into my shirt pocket. Just then, Elizabeth called out to her sister. Sheila turned and followed her toward the door. I'll talk to Sister Phillip later. I don't believe anything Sheila says and I can't believe Cecilia would run away from Regina.

That's the first thing I had read that made sense. I turned the page but it was blank. *You knew the truth, Karl? Why didn't you write it down? You died that day and the truth was buried with you.* I shivered as I realized I had read the last words Karl Bauer wrote. A few hours later, he was dead on the library floor. A deep sigh escaped me as I picked up the faxes and continued reading the bios. I shivered again as a name and a face slowly began forming in my mind. I would have seen it sooner if all the confusion and fear of these last days hadn't driven logic from my mind. I would have understood immediately if the names weren't always different. I knew who killed Cecilia and Karl. I was in his house.

Chapter Twenty-four

The Walsh library wasn't where I wanted to be. I was about to accuse my best friend's uncle of the fifty-year-old murder of two people. The irony was that one of his victims had been my aunt. It was all in the report. His excellent academics at Harvard, his distinguished career in service, winning medal after medal for bravery, heroism, 'without any thought for his own life' one citation read. The report continued with his brilliant law career and subsequent unblemished political life. He had come home a hero and married the best friend of the fiancée who had jilted him three years before. Only she hadn't jilted him. He had murdered her.

What a rags to riches story. Son of a bricklayer, Thomason Richard Walsh, Tommy to his friends, a cold-blooded killer. He had killed Karl to cover up my aunt's murder. He had probably married Karen's aunt just to make sure his connection with Cecilia never seemed suspicious. Poor Shelly married to someone who undoubtedly never loved her. Sister A was killed because she was starting to remember and he couldn't risk that. Now, he viewed me as a risk. Myriad thoughts swirled in my mind like fallen leaves twisting in a capricious wind.

Karen's voice intruded. "Gracie, Aunt Shelly left her evening bag. I'm going to run it over now and finish my make-up there. Be back as soon as I can." The door was closing on her last words.

I burst into movement. "Wait!" I yelled. She was gone. The Walsh home was adjacent to the college. It backed up to the northwest corner of the property. I remembered catching a glimpse of the house through winter-bare trees. It was visible from the Grotto.

I moved toward the door to chase after Karen. She'd probably cut around behind the house to save time. Maybe not. She was wearing high heels. I needed to get to Ric and tell him. Tell him what? The same thing I was going to tell Karen? Their uncle was a murderer! My pace slowed as the rest of the logic I refused to acknowledge started seeping into my brain and spreading like an indelible stain. I stopped.

My brain began to numb as full realization settled over me. Richard surely killed two people in 1941. He couldn't have held a pillow over Sister A's head. He was too frail himself. Sister Andrew could have taken *him* down. He couldn't have driven the car that side swiped me; he didn't drive anymore. Who set the fire to avoid discovery of the trunks? Who knew I had them in my car? Who learned everything I learned, as I learned it? The parking pass. Harry had seen it in the Rover, but I had one in my purse. "Oh God," the words slipped out in a whisper.

"Mrs. Marsden, are you all right?" His voice was soft and concerned, but all I saw was the specter of evil that had murdered two people. "I'm glad to have an opportunity to talk to you alone." He continued. "It's important that we wait here. I've called the college and asked Ric to come back. It will be over soon."

I couldn't believe my ears! Was this evil old man asking me to wait patiently while he and his nephew took care of one more loose end? I assumed that Ric would come through the front. I took off across the hallway, through the kitchen and towards where I hoped the back door would be. It was. My hand was turning the knob when I heard Uncle Richard yelling for me to stop.

"Wait, wait it's over. It must be over!"

Not for me you bastard, I thought as I ran down the steps. Damn. The night was pitch black. My best bet was to reach the college and the safety in numbers. A few yards away from the lights of the house, I began to grope my way. That slowed me down, but I figured I had time since no one was after me. I was wrong.

"Grace." His voice was low, tense, and too close.

I froze, afraid to breathe lest he heard me. I crouched behind the rocks at the back of the Grotto. He passed within a few yards of me. I heard noises all around me. *Oh God, Harry, why didn't I listen to you?* My thoughts were jumbled, my arms and legs like lead. I needed to get to the college. I could see the lights, but I was afraid to cross all that distance. The science building would be locked. It was too much ground to cover. Suddenly, I remembered the old chapel gate to the Sisters' Garden. It was twenty yards or so to my left. I could go through the garden to the tunnels and come up in Powers Hall. At least I'd be inside. If the tunnel was still open. If the gate wasn't locked. If Ric wasn't ten yards to my left waiting for me to move. I couldn't crouch there all night. I stood slowly and listened. Soft sounds from my right reached my ears.

Good, I thought. That would leave me free to reach the gate. I moved across the ground quickly and quietly. I stumbled once. When I thought I was close to the gate, I dropped to my knees and began to crawl. I was trying to feel along the bottom of the gate to push up the peg and make sure nothing obstructed it from swinging open. My hands touched metal! It wasn't locked. The gate moved under my tentative push, but not without a protest. The long un-oiled metal sounded a loud grinding complaint. I heard a movement nearby that made my decision for me. I squeezed through the rest of the way leaving the gate open, hoping Ric couldn't identify the noise he must have heard. I moved forward into the tunnels, confused about which way to go. Again, a noise prompted me to action. It sounded like a thump like something dropping to the ground. I inched down the tunnel. The gate didn't sound the alarm, but I knew someone was down here with me. I moved faster, surer, following the tunnel to a double door. *Thank God*, I thought as I turned the knob. It didn't move. The tunnel ended in a kind of *cul de sac* with three sets of double doors. I couldn't go back, I could sense soft steps in the tunnel behind me. The next handle remained fixed. My thoughts were frantic. *I can turn and face him. What chance would I have? His hands have caressed me, now they could easily snap my neck!* I was panicking, my hands reached for my last chance. The silent prayer on my lips turned into a *'thank you God,'* as the knob gave under my hand and the door opened. I slipped inside quickly, and turned to run up the one and a half flight of stairs to safety. Instead, I fell over a chair and then a couch. I was not in Power basement. As my eyes grew accustomed to the dark, I realized I was in the Fine Arts basement. Probably in the props room. I stepped carefully around stools, trunks, and theater paraphernalia. I was surrounded by tables, wooden and metal signs, a faded billboard, racks of clothes from a Greek toga to Miss Adelaide's skin tight gown from her nightclub sizzler, "Take Back Your Pearls." A wistful smile tugged a corner of my mouth as I remembered the fun we had staging the musical,

Guys and Dolls almost twenty years ago. I shrugged off the memory and picked my way around a Victorian settee, its original splendor threadbare and neglected. The props room was next to the lighting and audio chambers. I heard a noise from the hallway side of the door and moved quickly to hide behind a piece of scenery. My eyes were focused on the door and the wait seemed interminable. Sneezing became a dangerous possibility. My movements had disturbed years old dust. I crouched in the dark and wondered if this was how my aunt had spent the last minutes of her life. Had she been hiding from Tommy, hoping his footsteps would pass her by? Was she killed where he found her or left to die in the wall?

I shivered in revulsion. I shivered again as I realized that the fear motivated body heat of a minute before had left me. The room was cold and damp. A low noise from inside the room began to fill my head and I carefully lowered myself to a sitting position. The temperature dropped more it seemed and I clasped my arms around my knees to keep my shaking limbs from revealing my position. *She must be here,* I thought to myself. *I've followed her footsteps. Will her fate be mine?* My mind filled with thoughts, events. Not mine. My eyes replayed a long since played out scene from another time, exactly fifty years ago to the day. Another life. Her life.

Tommy quietly closed the Chapel Garden gate and entered the tunnel. He had achieved his objective. He was officially engaged to the Honorable Judge Clemens daughter, Sandra. She was enthralled; her father relieved that his less than attractive daughter would be married. Tommy and the Judge came to a gentlemen's agreement. The news would be in the papers next week. A stunning June wedding with all the right people in attendance was planned. Tommy felt some remorse at his treatment of Cecilia. She really was a sweet and trusting girl. Somewhere in the tiny part of his heart that was still decent, he felt a great regret for his actions. He reached the dumbwaiter and climbed aboard. He was working the pulleys and thinking of how he would tell her that it was over. He made a cavalier decision and decided to tell her first and not try to have her one more time. Her eagerness to please him in their lovemaking and his lust for sex had made for a great combination as far as he was concerned. Tommy had bragged to John many times about his sex with her. John wouldn't believe him. Tommy had bemoaned the awful sex he suffered with Sandra. John did believe that. He often joked with Tommy that he was relieved that he didn't have to sleep with her. Tommy had promised John that he'd work it out so he could watch him and Cecilia one night. This was to be a form of payback to John for his introduction to Sandra Clemens. His decision was made. He'd tell her first. He knew she'd cry and after he consoled her he'd make love to her one more time; a kind of good-bye. Too bad about John, he'd let him watch with Sandra. Knowing that John was watching might make it exciting. Conscience cleared, he climbed out of the dumbwaiter and turned expectantly. Cecilia wasn't there. She must have lifted the latch and stepped back to her room. No matter, he knew the way in the dark. Tommy opened the door to Cecilia's room and stepped inside. He saw her stretched out across her bed. He smiled thinking she must be exhausted after her duties of the day. Again, a pang of regret that someone so beautiful and sweet should have no useful family registered in his mind. He lifted a blanket from the foot of the bed to cover her when he noticed her dress. The gown was unlike anything he'd ever seen on Cecilia. Even her finest outfit was no match for this apparel. As he wondered about her dress, he noticed the open book on her bureau. He could barely read it by the dim light from the burning lamp. He reached for the book, his heart beginning to race. 'The stupid bitch' he swore under his breath. Cecilia's sleep was light and Tommy's voice awakened her. Because of the near darkness, Cecilia couldn't see the scowl on his face. She only knew he was near. Suddenly, she realized she was still in her gown. Quickly she sprang up from the bed and backed toward her closet across the room. She believed it would be bad luck for the groom to see the bride in her wedding dress before the ceremony. It would be. Tommy reached her side in two quick strides. He grabbed her wrist and waved the book in her face. "What are you doing? Do you want to ruin me? I told you not to tell. Oh God, this could ruin me." Cecilia was astounded at his reaction. "'Tommy, I know I wasn't to tell, but I couldn't reach you and after I saw the doctor and found out, I knew you would understand why I had to tell and I..." Cecilia's voice ran down to a tiny whisper and stopped altogether. Tommy's face turned white as the realization of what she was babbling came to him. He had to know.

"What did you find out?" he asked in a harsh voice she barely recognized. She never expected this response. She knew he'd be surprised, but she thought he'd be pleased. Tommy's tone filled her with fear.

"What did you find out?" each word terse and clipped. "Tommy, please don't be angry. I know it's a surprise, but a baby is a gift from God."

"No!" he roared with an intensity that shocked her. He pushed her away from him as though that action could push this nightmare away from his carefully plotted reality. Cecilia tumbled backward. Her head hit the corner of the marble washstand as she fell. She was still.

Tommy turned away after the initial shove. He was muttering that 'things would have to be done, he'd find a doctor, he'd pay for everything, it'd be okay' Tommy, expecting protests from Cecilia, turned at her silence. "Oh my God!" Before he touched her, before he tilted her head to the side and revealed the ugly bruise on her temple, he knew she was dead! The sparkle that had emanated from her happy soul and shone through her eyes had dulled, leaving only sightless orbs like a fogged crystal on a broken watch.

The cold and fear must have caused an almost fugue-like state. I wasn't crouched behind a fake skyscraper anymore. I was standing upright next to a door I'd never noticed before. Another noise in the hall prompted me to open the door. *Okay, this is more like it.* There seemed to be a small glow from some equipment that must remain charged. Maybe generators. I closed the door behind me and moved toward the panel. I took a few cautious steps when I heard the door open. *Stupid*! I didn't even try to lock it. I lunged forward, hoping to turn something on or off; something that would tell someone I was down here. I lurched sideways and realized that I had snagged the piece of yarn tied off on my jeans belt loop around the curlicue arm of a metal chair. I lost precious time as I wiggled the yarn off the metal. I headed again for the panel. My fingers had barely brushed some knobs when a strong arm grabbed me from behind. The arm around my neck was cutting off my air, strangling me. "Ric," my voice was already hoarse, "don't!" I tried to kick, but I was off balance and pulled backwards. My fingers, ineffective, pulled at the arm. The arm! It was bare, smooth. *Oh God, Karen,* I thought as the arm tightened even more. My knees were weak and buckled. The lights on the panel were blurring. Her grip lessened just a little. I allowed myself to slump more. The grip loosened a little. This was my only chance. The arms that I had let go limp at my side now snapped up to grab her arm. I pulled her forward and bucked back against her to throw her off balance. It worked. She tried to tighten her hold but she was off balance. I broke free and ran to the door. My knees, still weak, couldn't hold me. I stumbled and then went down on all fours. I shook my head from side to side. The exertion took its toll. I couldn't focus. A gasping sound, intensifying to a growl, forced my head up. I saw a pair of shoes. I saw the statuette, a bronze cherub with a twisted, hideous smile, and in a slow-motion second I realized how a person five feet, seven inches tall could strike a blow from the height of six feet, two inches. Her victim had been on his knees! Shelly Walsh loomed above me, an unholy light burning in her eyes. She was holding the statue above her head, poised to repeat history! The statue crashed to the floor inches from my head and rolled up against the dusty wall. I imagined that the crack I heard had been the statue splitting my skull, but the deafening sound was the report from a gun fired in close quarters.

"No, Uncle Richard!" Ric's scream had been too late.

"Mrs. Marsden, are you all right?" A gentle voice at my elbow asked. He helped me as I struggled to my feet.

"I'm okay," a shaky, hoarse voice answered from inside me. Lights came on from every corner. My eyes hurt in the strong light. More voices, footsteps running.

"Grace, Grace!" Harry's voice, strong and close. Soon he was at my side. "Harry" a croak escaped my throat.

"Darling, are you all right?" His eyes searched my face for reassurance. I nodded and flung myself against his body. His arms folded around me and for the first time that evening, I felt safe. Tears stung my eyes as relief flooded my body. I turned to face Ric and his uncle. The older man stood quietly, almost shrinking before my eyes, so frail and somehow lost. Ric gently removed the pistol from his uncle's hand and guided him to a chair. In the midst of the confusion, my brain registered two sounds; distant sirens and an earsplitting scream. Karen had raced in behind Harry and now stood staring at a spot behind me. I followed her eyes to those of a dead woman. Shelly Walsh lay crumpled on the floor in the corner where we had struggled. Her eyes were open, unseeing, staring up at an angle on the wall. I followed her lifeless gaze to that spot on the wall. For an instant, a blink of a weary eye, I saw a faint outline. Harry tightened his arm around me as he felt my body tremble. Shelly was killed instantly by the single shot that entered the center of her forehead. Harry turned me away and led me from the room. Ric was comforting Karen much the same way. Only Uncle Richard sat quietly but not calmly. His eyes, as lackluster as his dead wife's, stared around the room.

"I had to stop her. She knew," he began quietly. "I didn't know until later. She knew," he repeated. He was thrusting his hand over his hair, pushing a lock from his forehead. I knew that habit. It was Ric's. I had seen him push his hair off his forehead that way a hundred times. It was strange to see that exact motion made by another hand.

"Uncle Richard, don't say anything more until you have your attorney present," Ric advised. He stood directly in front of his uncle and tried to make eye contact. Karen's plaintive whisper, "Uncle Richard, why?" distracted Ric. In that moment, Richard grabbed the gun from Ric's waistband.

He leapt from his chair pushing Karen into Ric and backed away from them slowly raising the pistol to his head. The sirens reached a crescendo; I could barely hear Ric pleading. "No, Uncle Richard, don't!"

For the second time that night, the sharp crack of a firearm rang out. Richard dropped to the floor, like a marionette whose strings had been slashed.

CHAPTER TWENTY-FIVE

The shock of that night remained with everyone who had witnessed the scene in that death chamber. The police inquest, the funeral, everything connected with that night, seemed surreal. I moved through the events in a state of slow motion. The only fact I knew was that I didn't feel my aunt's presence any longer. I didn't "see" film in my head or fall into a fugue any more. She was finally at peace.

The police had managed to glean the entire story of that evening from everyone's statements. Ric had confirmed that his uncle had called him at Regina demanding that he come back immediately; telling him that I was in danger. It had taken the switchboard several minutes to locate him to take the phone call. Ric hadn't even tried to find his aunt; he had just left. He thought his aunt was at the college. She had told him she wanted to mingle during the reception. At one point he spotted her talking to Karen, but he soon lost sight of her and lost interest in her agenda. When Ric returned to the house, he had found his uncle in a panic gesturing toward the back door. Richard kept telling Ric, "She's out there alone. She thinks it's me. You've got to find her before she does!" Ric didn't understand his uncle's babbling, but he understood that I was out there, alone and in danger.

I had left word at the hospital earlier for Harry that I would be spending the night at Karen's. He had called to 'tuck me in'. Karen had left her phone on call forwarding earlier that day, so Harry's call came to Richard's house. Harry identified himself to the very frantic voice of Richard Walsh.

"Mr. Marsden, come quickly. Your wife is in terrible danger. Ric has gone after her!"

Harry rushed from hospital ignoring the doctor's protest. A quick call to Walter had a car and driver outside Good Samaritan. Harry told the police he had spent the entire drive to River Forest urging Walter to drive faster and agonizing over Richard's statement that 'Ric has gone after her!' Harry had asked Walter to bring a gun with him. Walter had quietly handed him a Colt .38. No questions asked. Harry held the Colt clumsily in his left hand, cursing his bandaged right fingers. He knew he'd have to get close to be accurate.

Both Ric and Harry told the police that neither one of them was any too sure of whom they were after. Ric's account said he had followed Richard's gesture toward the back of the property. At one point, he thought he heard me, and he called out softly. Apparently, that alerted Shelly that he was out there.

When I had pushed open the gate, Ric had been close enough to hear the grind. He said that he was crouched at the gate when he sensed someone behind him. He turned, but not quickly enough to avoid a blow from a good-sized rock. His body slumping to the ground was the thud I had heard in the tunnels. Ric's statement got a little fuzzy about what happened next. When he came to, he realized that the gate had been pushed wide open and that his 9-mm Glock was gone. He rushed through the tunnels arriving seconds before Richard fired. His scream to stop had frozen in his throat. He explained his hesitation.

"Mrs. Marsden was on the floor gasping for air, trying to

raise her arms to stop the bone crushing blow that would have certainly killed her. My aunt saw Richard point the gun at her and I thought she'd stop. Her eyes were like two burning black holes; her lips curved in a twisted smile and she turned back to Mrs. Marsden. I was too late."

Ric's shout and the gun's report were almost simultaneous. Ric guessed that his uncle had lost patience waiting at home. When he found Ric, unconscious, and the gate open, he must have known he needed to act quickly. He took the gun and followed a hauntingly familiar path.

Harry's description of his chase played like a nightmare in slow motion. Harry had raced up the stairs of the Walsh's home to find the lights on and the doors standing open. He ran out the back towards the glow of the college lights. He stumbled in the darkness, silently cursing his lack of foresight in not bringing a flashlight, when he spotted movement to his right. He recognized Ric's shape and saw him enter the garden. As Harry reached the gate, he heard the shot.

At this point during his statement, he had confessed to me with tears in his eyes. "Grace, I was terrified. I thought I was too late." Harry found the room moments after Richard Walsh saved my life.

Karen's account explained what had prompted the grisly events. She had spoken with her aunt briefly at the reception, and had innocently remarked that she had left me reading faxes and studying the handyman's journal. Karen told the police that her aunt had seemed upset and excused herself on the pretense of headache. She told Karen she needed to get away from the noise for a few minutes. Karen never saw her again. When people were being seated for dinner and Ric and her aunt were missing, Karen had become worried. She thought perhaps that her aunt's headache had worsened and that Ric had escorted her home. Karen's arrival on the heels of Harry entering the college prop room had completed the cast of characters for that evening's deadly performance. No one there that night would erase the memory of the final moments of two people bound by their secrets; a fifty year old legacy of violence and death.

CHAPTER TWENTY-SIX

A week after the funeral, Harry and I drove downtown to an attorney's office for the reading of Richard and Shelly Walsh's wills. The attorney was a partner in Richard Walsh's old law firm. Karen and Ric had entered the building ahead of us, and I didn't hurry my pace or call out to Karen. She had transferred partial blame for her aunt and uncle's deaths to me. Her bitterness and resentment towards me charged the air at their funeral. The funeral had been delayed two days longer than customary to give Ric a chance to recover from the wound he suffered that night. Ric had leaned heavily on the pulpit as he gave the eulogies for Richard and Shelly. He had been pale and unsteady on his feet, but he had insisted on doing it.

Ric had been injured when he lunged for his uncle to prevent his suicide. The bullet that killed Richard had almost killed Ric, smashing into his chest after ripping a course through the older man's head. Ric was on the way to a full recovery.

Karen's recovery was not as certain. She was filled with bitterness over the loss of the two people who she had considered parents. Karen was consumed with anger at the events, me, and even at her brother. During the funeral, she'd made it perfectly clear that our relationship was over.

My thoughts were on that lost friendship as we followed them into the building. Harry slowed his pace and we just missed sharing the elevator. I thought Karen caught a glimpse of me. The vacant look in her eyes cleared briefly as the doors closed.

A secretary confirmed our appointment and ushered us into a conference room. John Flynn approached us. "Good morning, Mr. Marsden, Mrs. Marsden. Thank you for coming."

"Mr. Flynn, I told you when you called that I didn't understand why my husband and I should be here. I still don't know why you want us here." My concern was that in a few minutes I'd have to walk through that connecting door and face a person I had called best friend up until two weeks ago.

"I understand your confusion, especially in view of the circumstances. Mr. Walsh added a codicil to his will in his own writing two days before he died instructing that you and your husband be present at the reading of his will."

Harry took my hand for added support as I switched a length of lavender yarn to my left hand.

"Right now," Mr. Flynn continued, "Mrs. Walsh's will is being read. If you'll make yourselves comfortable, I'll send my secretary when we're ready for you." John Flynn left the room via that connecting door.

Harry and I took seats opposite the door, like two people waiting for an interview for the same job.

"Shelly's will shouldn't take long, Love. It's probably very simple in that everything passes to Richard in the event of her death," Harry commented.

"Sure, how could she know her husband would kill her after she went crazy trying to protect him." My sarcasm annoyed Harry.

"Grace, if it weren't for Richard, we'd be hearing your last will and testament. I don't see why you can't appreciate that."

"Appreciate what? That he murdered my aunt! That because of him my mother anguished for years! Appreciate that he wasn't man enough to face his crimes!" Hot tears burned my eyes as I choked out the last words. "I hate him for what he did to my family and I'm glad he's dead!" I had twisted the pastel strands into a series of angry loops and knots during my tirade.

Harry looked away trying to defuse the moment. He knew that any conversation would be impossible for me. Flynn's secretary opened the door and motioned us inside.

A few feet into the room, I realized that the secretary was leaving and Flynn was making ready to do the same. He asked us to take the two seats that put us next to Ric and Karen. I hesitated and Harry walked in front of me to take the seat next to Ric. Only five feet separated Karen and me, but it might as well have been a lifetime. Actually, it was. She glanced at my left hand as I conspicuously shoved the distorted yarn down between my leg and the side of the chair.

"As I explained earlier," Flynn began, "Mr. Walsh instructed that the four of you be present to view his last will and testament."

We all looked surprised at the word 'view,' but his meaning was soon clear. John Flynn slid a videocassette into a VCR and asked that we join him in his office when we were finished.

Four pairs of eyes watched him leave after his mysterious announcement. As the door closed behind him, we were startled by the sound of Richard Walsh's voice! The tape started with the almost predictable opening line of, 'If you're watching this, I must be dead.'

Ric hit the stop button on the control and "froze" Richard on the screen. He turned to his sister who had slumped in her chair. "Karen, come on now. You don't have to watch this. Why don't you wait outside?"

"I think she should stay Kramer." Harry's voice startled me. "Your uncle had a purpose in wanting us all here."

"Shut up, Marsden!" Ric snapped. "Can't you see what this is doing to her?"

"That's why she's got to stay and find out why this all happened. That's the only way she'll get past this."

"Stop talking about me like I'm not in the room." Karen's weak voice grew stronger as she continued. "I want to stay. I was just surprised to see him again," she added quietly.

"That bastard Flynn could have warned us!" argued Ric.

Karen reached over and took the remote out of his hand. She released her uncle's frozen frame and in so doing allowed him an unburdening that was fifty years in the making.

"I don't mind dying. I've had enough time to live to know that. I hope this recording will explain; I know it can't excuse what I did. I wanted the four of you to see this together because your lives are connected in a strange way. Fifty years ago I seduced a lovely young girl named Cecilia. I was using her to pass away my summer. At the same time, I was trying to romance Sandra, Judge Cleman's daughter. The romance could further my career. The night I came to Cecilia's room, my intention was to end the relationship. I found out that night that she was pregnant. My dream world was spinning away from me! I pushed her away from me in anger, but I swear I never meant to kill her." His voice caught with emotion. He cleared his throat and continued. *"I've relived that night a thousand sleepless nights since then. Fear and panic overcame me. I couldn't be found there. I couldn't be ruined, now, when everything was falling into place, everything I'd worked so*

hard for. It wasn't easy pretending to love Sandra, caressing her lumpy body and pressing kisses on her homely face. What would happen now? In the next moment, I was remembering everything Cecilia had worked so hard for. She had come so far and had so many bright plans for her future. I began to cry as I looked at her slender body crumpled and still at my feet.

"A noise in the hallway brought me back. Had someone heard and reported the commotion? Were the police on their way now? Were they outside the door? Panic gripped me again, harder. I quickly walked to the bureau and extinguished the lamp. I carefully opened the door and viewed the hallway. No one was out there. The room was illuminated by the full moon. A plan formed in my mind. I knew Cecilia kept a valise at the back of her closet. I quickly emptied the bureau drawers into the large soft-sided valise. Stop thinking, just move, I told my brain. In my hurry, I apparently missed the crumpled papers in the wastebasket and the single sheet of paper tucked under some undergarments. Satisfied that I had stuffed her meager belongings into the bag, I paused to think things through. I knew I had to work quickly. I wasn't sure of anything. The moon was too bright to risk carrying the body out to my car. I'd have to cover too much open, snow-bright ground. I was afraid to carry the body all the way out to the grotto through the underground. This was Saturday night, the most popular night for its use. More than once, I had passed young men in the tunnels, averting my eyes, yet raising a hand in silent salute. I couldn't risk that either.

"Finally, the rest of my plan took shape. I'd take the body out into the hallway for the short thirty feet to the back stairs that led to the nun's entrance to the Chapel. I figured the nuns were in bed and asleep by now. This route seemed safer than bumping into clandestine lovers in the tunnels. I knew about

the dedication of the new library tomorrow. My father's company had the contract to do the fireplace in that room. The firebox on that was huge and the cavern behind it would be perfect for concealing Cecilia's body. The chapel was adjacent to the new library. This route would give me the best cover. First, I needed to dispose of the valise. I decided to carry that through the tunnels as I had at the beginning of one of our weekends together. I fastened the straps, and lifted it and heard a soft crackle. I looked down. A piece of crumpled writing paper had missed its target and rolled to the middle of the room. I reached down and read one of Cecilia's attempts to her Aunt Fiona.

"Oh God, how many of these were around? I reached for the basket and stuffed the contents into my pockets. I groped around on the floor to find any other errant attempts and even ran my hand under the bed. Satisfied I had all the copies, I put the first one I found in the wastebasket. It said nothing of a baby. Let people think she left me at the altar. I assumed the nuns and several classmates already knew about the wedding. I knew the relationship Cecilia referred to in the letter was college; let everyone else think it referred to me. I would find a way to fix things with Sandra and the Judge. Better to be accused of sowing wild oats than committing murder.

"I was feeling quite confident with my quickly conceived plan as I carried the valise out the Chapel Garden and towards the back of the grotto where my car was parked. By the time I returned I was positively inflated with how well his plan was working. By now, the lawyer in me was trying to justify the events. Even the sight of Cecilia's lifeless body ceased to upset me. I became very bold, and decided to carry the body in my arms without a cover or blanket. After all, why draw attention to a missing blanket? Anyway, carrying a concealed bundle *might prompt questions. I thought all this through as I carefully lifted her into my arms, making sure I carried her with the damaged side of her head toward my chest. I had brought a polishing rag from my car to protect my clothes. She really did look asleep. If I were seen, a student might ignore the indiscretion of apparent overindulgence of gin and tonic, thinking, 'There but for the grace of God go I.'*

"I opened the door with my right hand and carefully stepped into the hallway. The gaslights seemed to sputter and then brighten, like torches illuminating every corner. Long-gone panic began to return. I swallowed hard and moved quickly across the short corridor to the doorway. The doorknob wouldn't turn! Fear mounted in my mind. My heart began to pound; so much so that for a moment I thought I felt a heartbeat from the corpse I carried. I nearly dropped her and ran, but just then my sweaty palm made better contact with the knob, it turned under my hand and I entered the passageway. Once inside, I leaned against the wall, my panic subsiding. I felt the sweat streaming from my armpits down the inside of my shirt. 'Don't be an ass, Walsh,' I spoke aloud to assure myself of my control. I quickly passed through the Chapel into the library. The full moon still acted as my accomplice. I could see well enough to move to the fireplace. I placed the body on the floor and tried to peer into the hole. I'd have to work by feel here since even the moonlight couldn't penetrate the crypt-like darkness. I knew from an earlier conversation with my brother Kevin that the fireplace wasn't finished. Kevin had told me that Dad had two men scheduled to be at Regina at 6:00 a.m. to complete the job. 'Lazy day workers' is what Kevin had said. This would be easier than I thought. Rather than carry their supplies to and from the job, my father's crew had left their tools and materials in a neat pile next to the fireplace. I

carried some tools in my trunk but now I didn't have to risk another trip and leave her lying in the open.

"I sneered at what they would think when they arrived in the morning to do the job and it was already done. I knew they wouldn't report it. They'd agree to cheat my father and put down the time on their cards.

"I struggled with my conscience and my stomach again. Big as the cavity was, it was difficult to handle her body into it. People don't fold easily and dead people don't even lift easily. My nerves were stretched tight and the thought of having to break her lifeless limbs to get her into the hole made me nauseous. I knew I was next to the chapel. Maybe I should have gone into the sanctuary and begged for forgiveness. I hadn't meant to kill her. I looked back and forth. The chapel with the faint glimmer of the perpetual light visible through the stained glass panel in the door offered a chance at retribution and forgiveness. The gaping, black hole filled with cold guaranteed concealment and escape.

"I was weak. My cheeks were wet with sweat and tears as I prepared to try again. I knew I could never smash the flesh that had been warm and scented just an hour ago. Even now, I could smell Lily of the Valley on my clothes. I lifted her and half leaned into the yawning cavern to stuff the body into the cavity. For a brief moment, maybe a second, or two, I felt trapped by the hole! In those brief moments that seem to last an eternity, I feared that God was reaching out to punish me. The terror grew as I thought of being buried alive, dying slowly and painfully; the only witness the sightless corpse I clutched. I choked back a scream and pushed Cecilia's body with a terror-fed strength that propelled me backward out of the cold, marble hole.

"My heart was racing, my breathing jagged. I knew I was

losing control. I knew I had to brick up the hole fast. I wanted to slap up the wall with the fastest design I knew, but I reasoned that a last minute change in design would be suspicious. I carried the spec sheet over to the window to see the design. An angular horseshoe shape with eleven rows. Because of the design, I needed to cut several bricks. I muffled the sound with my heavy overcoat, careful to contain the flying chips within my new Chesterfield, a gift from Sandra.

"I had taken some deep breaths and tried to calm down. The ability to block out my deed slowly returned as I gathered materials and began a craft I had learned as a child. Slow and awkward at first, I regained the speed and dexterity of summers past until I settled into a rhythm, trowel, set, trowel, set. The rhythm of scrapes and taps the only sound besides my measured breathing. Trowel, set, trowel, set. No remorse, no fear, only efficiency, and a growing wall to conceal a horrible tragedy. Already my mind was absolving me of guilt and reshaping the earlier events at arms' length. I could tell by the touch that the mortar was even and smooth. I had good hands when it came to this sort of thing. Too bad my father had encouraged higher goals for me. Maybe I would have been happier joining my dad and older brother in the family business. I picked up the overcoat. I needed no coat against the cold my body was still boiling from the night's events. I'd go home now and try to sleep. I was supposed to attend the dedication tomorrow with my father and brother. I tried not to think about how it would feel to be in this room. All the prominent families would be there. There would be questions if I didn't attend. We were joining the Conners for tea at the college later. I never like being around Elizabeth Conners. Ours had been a romance that turned ugly and vindictive. She had glimpsed a darker side of me fueled by sex and alcohol. I

felt exposed when she looked at me.

"I shook off those disturbing thoughts. I reached my car and drove off believing that I had unintentionally committed the perfect crime. Every first year law student knew that there could be no crime without a body.

"That is the memory I've lived with each night of my life. I panicked. I couldn't be ruined. I was so scared. Believe me though, Mrs. Marsden, she was dead. If there had been a chance to save her, I would have, even if it meant I'd pay the price. I'm not a murderer!"

Again, he halted his narrative to clear his throat. *"Am I now?"* The irony of his anguished question filled the pause. *"The next day at the dedication, I noticed Karl Bauer, the college handyman snooping around the fireplace. I chatted with my father's friends but my insides were twisted in a knot. I waited until most of the guests had gone before I approached the fireplace. I must have stood there for several minutes. I was the only one in the library. I ran my hand along the smooth marble, fingering the inscription, wondering what Karl had noticed.*

"'Looking for these?' Karl's voice had startled me. He held out his hand and showed me some of the beads from her dress. He had found them on the floor near the fireplace. I told him I didn't know what he was talking about. 'You don't know what I'm talking about?' His voice mocked me. 'Then maybe you know about Cecilia's going off so quickly,' he asked me. 'I just found out myself. I expected to see her today at the ceremony and I'm told that she's gone off and left a half scribbled note ending our relationship. What would you expect me to know? How do you expect me to feel? I just got home last night.' I thought my protests sounded genuine. His eyebrows tightened at my last comment and I knew that my

perfect crime was crumbling. I tried to wave him off and walk away, but he grabbed by hand. He saw that my hand was raw and scraped. He looked from me to the fireplace and the expression of pure horror that spread over his face told me he knew. My brain exploded. I panicked and sucker punched him. He staggered back against the bookcase. I took off like a bat out of hell. I drove around for hours until I finally went home to pack some things. It was there that I heard the news about Pearl Harbor. The police hadn't been around looking for me yet. I couldn't figure out why, but I wasn't taking any chances. I told my father and brother I had enlisted. I left that night to join the Army and to begin a lifetime of lies and regret.

"I could never understand why Bauer hadn't called the police until I received a letter from Sheila Conner filling me in on the news from home. She sent some clippings from the River Forest Gazette. In a small paragraph, I read the reason why the police never came for me. Karl Bauer died in a tragic accident when a statuette on a high shelf toppled and smashed his skull. 'Tragic accident.' I knew the truth. I had inadvertently killed two people in as many days. I was devastated. I'd never meant for any of that to happen. All those medals I received? I wasn't trying to be a hero; I was trying to die! I was too much a coward to kill myself. I was hoping the enemy would do it for me.

"Sheila persisted with her letters to me. At first, I was thankful for the contact. After several months of writing, her tone began to change. She began to talk about plans for after the war, plans that mentioned the two of us. A short six months before, I would have played along and used her affection to get through the war and then ignore her when I got stateside. I always knew she had a huge crush on me. I couldn't do that anymore. I wrote and told her how I felt. Her next letter to me

turned my nightmare into a living hell!

"She had found the letter Cecilia had written home explaining about the baby and naming me as the father. She told me not to be so quick to write her off unless I wanted my father and brother to be humiliated with the story. What would the police think about Cecilia's disappearance then? I renewed my efforts to get killed in combat, but I returned home a hero.

"Mr. Conners, Sheila's father, was waiting to take me into his law firm when I returned. Sheila was waiting to take me to the altar. I was tired; I didn't care. We were married.

"Several years into our futile marriage, I asked Sheila for a divorce. I never wanted her in the way a man should want his wife. It seemed that anytime I came close to touching her, I'd think of Cecilia and the secret I hid. I started using my middle name. I told people that Richard sounded better for business. Truth is, I couldn't stand to hear the name Tommy anymore. It reminded me of how Cecilia would say my name, all breathless and hopeful at the same time.

"Sheila flew into a rage calling me ungrateful and common. It was during one of these tirades, that she let slip something that turned me against her with more hatred and contempt then I had ever felt for anyone. She knew about Cecilia! She had known since the day in the library. She came back to find me. She overhead Karl accuse me of killing Cecilia and sealing her in the wall. Her slip was mentioning hearing Karl muttering to himself about calling the police. I am not proud of what I did next, but I had to know. I beat her until she admitted that she had picked up the statuette from the floor where it had fallen and she had delivered the deathblow! She described how Karl had slumped to the floor after he had slammed into the bookcase and that the statuette had rolled to within inches of where she was standing. Karl was on his

knees when she approached him with the smiling cherub held over her head. She said he heard a noise and started to raise his head. He never saw the statue that crushed his skull. All those years I carried that guilt with me. I remember her face twitched wildly and blood streamed from her nose where I had punched her. She glared at me with burning eyes that seared my soul. She screamed, 'We are bound to each other by our sins. I'll see you in hell before I let you go!' She laughed hysterically, spume dripping from her swollen lip and I knew in that moment that she was right. We belonged to each other in our vileness. I vowed then not to leave her as my way of keeping her from harming anyone else. I deserved her. I knew she was evil.

"On that day, our relationship underwent a metamorphosis. I allowed her my name, my fortune, and all the things it could buy. She bought the house in Palm Springs, changed her name to Shelly to identify her new persona, and joined two country clubs. I moved into another bedroom. I also allowed her all the discreet affairs she wanted, for I wanted no part of her. Thank God, when I ran for office, the press never looked very far behind the candidate. We could never have survived today's political scrutiny.

"For years, we pretended a lie, for the truth was too heinous. Then, Mrs. Marsden, Karen brought you home. After a time, I realized that Cecilia Doyle had been your aunt.

"I could never look at you and not think of Cecilia. You didn't resemble her. Thank God for that. You had some mannerisms that reminded me of her. When Ric came to me and asked for my help in finding your husband, I called in every marker I had   to unravel the red tape to secure his release. I owed you.

"Years went by and I felt complacent in my life of lies.

Then, Cecilia was found. When I heard the first reports, I was sick all over again with the guilt and shame of what I had done. I even told Sheila that maybe this was destiny giving me another chance to set straight the record. I am afraid that my conversation with Sheila caused the events that followed. Karen and Ric spoke freely about the case and your involvement Mrs. Marsden. Sheila was obsessed with her prominence in the community and feared exposure much more than I did. Again, I was a coward and I did nothing. I didn't realize how crazy she was until the second attempt on your life. I thought a drunken driver had forced you off the road.

"I learned that Karen and Sheila had talked with Sister Andrew. I remembered that you were here the night you told Karen about the trunks. Slowly, I began to understand that Sheila's slide from reality could no longer be controlled.

"I don't know the circumstances of my death. My hope is that the four of you are viewing this confession and that Sheila and I are both dead. I've left other tapes with alternate instructions. I don't know who is listening to this twisted story, but the truth needs to be told to give some peace to those I've left behind. And maybe peace for me."

The last line was barely audible, spoken in hush like a prayer to a higher judge. The voice stopped. The face continued to stare at us from the screen, pleading for understanding, his mute supplication more powerful than any words. Then his face was gone.

About the Author

A native of the Chicago area and owner of her own staffing services corporation, Luisa Buehler attended Regina College during the seventies and graduated with a B.A. in English. Even then, the stories of spirits, sightings, and the supernatural intrigued her. Since then she has spent time 'giving back' to her community by volunteering as a Docent at Brookfield Zoo and as a trained leader in the Boy Scouts of America. With her debut novel, she has realized a dream that has been on hold while raising her son and running her company. Luisa lives in Lisle, Illinois with her husband, Gerry, their son, Christopher, and the family cat, Martin Marmalade. In her free time, Luisa loves to garden and wishes she could play golf better.

The PLOT
KATHLEEN
LAMARCHE

Three months before the Presidential election, reporter Cassandra Hart receives an urgent phone call from her father, a renowned journalist, who is on the verge of exposing a plot that will influence the election and change the course of history.

When Cassandra is forced to assume the quest, she races against time in a world of deception, intrigue, and murder.

As those she trusts are killed, discredited, and otherwise taken from her, Cassandra is increasingly isolated, but determined to expose the betrayal, unaware that her influential godfather is equally determined to stop her. Except for the help of Washington, D.C. detective Max Henshaw, she alone stands between democracy and the new world order.

ISBN 1-59080-203-9

MARC VUN KANNON

The Flame in the Bowl

Unbinding the Stone

"Not your usual, run-of-the-mill tale of saving the world from dark magics but something considerably more original!"
--Tanya Huff, author of *The Better Part of Valor*

Young Tarkas, a Singer of humble roots, whose worst crime had been accidentally stumbling upon a village elder and his wife..um...in the act, suddenly finds himself exiled from the only home he's ever known. Because of a flame in the bowl.

What Tarkas soon learns is that his misfortune is necessary to the future of the universe as he knows it. For he has been chosen as a Hero-in-training, and he must save the world.

With the aid of his new companions, one a Demi-God in disguise, the other a beast ferocious beyond compare (and a little help from the Elixir of Warrior), Tarkas uses his wit, strength, and Songs to track down the rogue Lords Elemental, restoring order to the realms that hang in the balance.

ISBN 1-59080-140-7

To order, visit our web catalog at
http://www.echelonpress.com/catalog/

Or ask your local bookseller!

BLAIR WING
HOUSE of CARDS

"4 ½ Roses! Sensual, steamy and passionate."
--A Romance Review

Sydney Rawlins is on the run with nowhere to go and no one to trust. Her brother is accused of murder and presumed dead, and a priceless piece of 200 year old art is missing. Refusing to give up hope, Sydney will do whatever it takes to find the truth even if it means losing her heart--and possibly her life--to a man with too many faces.

Graham Montgomery is not who he appears to be and the fewer people who know this, the better. Betrayal leads him on a dangerous journey to find peace with his life and past. With ties to both sides of the law, he has no time to waste protecting a headstrong woman determined to get herself killed in the name of justice.

The bright lights of the Vegas set a backdrop for intrigue and betrayal in a world of politics and art where no one will come out unscathed.

ISBN 1-59080-187-3

To order, visit our web catalog at
http://www.echelonpress.com/catalog/

Or ask your local bookseller!

CRUMBS IN THE KEYBOARD

Stories From Courageous Women Who Juggle Life & Writing

"This is wonderful!"
--Fern Michaels, New York Times best selling author

Eighty authors come together with words of wisdom, encouragement, humor, and true-life stories of what it is like to juggle the demands of a career and maintaining relationships with those around them. Each author is donating 100% of her royalties from the sale of Crumbs to The Center for Women and Families in Louisville, Kentucky. Echelon Press is matching those monies dollar for dollar. By purchasing Crumbs, you will help in the fight against domestic violence.

ISBN 1-59080-096-6

To order, visit our web catalog at
http://www.echelonpress.com/catalog/

Or ask your local bookseller!

Printed in the United States
1301100007B/13-27